Blood Bound

By

V. J. Devereaux

Table of Contents

Blood Bound - Copyright - 2013 Valerie Douglas writing as V. J. Devereaux

Cover art by JK Graphics

WITH THE EXCEPTION of quotes used in reviews, this book may not be reproduced or used in whole or in part by any means existing without written permission from the author.

Discover other titles by V. J. Devereaux

The Bound Series

Blood Bound – Book One

Magic Bound – Book Two

The Book of Demons series

Demon's Kiss

Demon's Embrace

Cherry's Jubilee

Dedication

To the inspiration for Julian and Nico, who shall both go unnamed, my thanks

Chapter One

NICHOLAS WALKED INTO the darkened library, scanning the room for his cousin. He found Julian standing in the opened French doors staring out over the vineyards, arms folded, his shoulder propped against the jamb. Beyond him, Nico could see the grapevines on their supports tipped with the last gilded rays of the setting sun, brilliant in comparison to the darkness of the room around them. That warm light illuminated his cousin's face and form as he stood brooding in the doorway, his dark head bowed a little.

Looking at him, as always Nico could almost understand the attraction some men felt for another man, although that was not his way, nor was it Julian's.

His cousin was tall, well-built, with a strong, handsome face. As a boy, Nico had thought him a giant, at least until he'd grown into his own height. He smiled a little at the memory but his smile faded as he studied the man who was not just his cousin but his closest friend.

The truth was Julian was lonely and had been lonely for a long time. As was Nico.

Money, they'd found, could isolate one even in a crowd.

It didn't help that circumstances had added a new weight to Julian's shoulders. Nico couldn't understand such unreasoning hate from those who didn't know him or them.

Julian didn't need to hear about that now, he needed a distraction. A pleasant one. He owed Julian a great deal and would have done much to ease his worries. This was a small thing.

"Julian," Nico said, and his cousin turned his head a little, his dark liquid eyes meeting Nico's.

Giving a seemingly careless shrug, Nico said, "Where's the harm? And there are advantages. You don't actually have to talk to them, only look. Who would expect a man like you to use such a pedestrian method to meet someone? Give it a try, it might be fun. If nothing else, we'll kill an hour or two."

He grinned at his cousin, who shook his head, but fought a smile of his own. As Nico had hoped.

Julian rolled his eyes at his cousin, fondly. He knew that engaging grin of old. It had gotten the younger man out of trouble many a time. As it likely would now. He sighed but worked hard at concealing a grin.

"What do you have to lose?" Nico added reasonably. "If you choose one, at the absolute worst you'll have a pleasant meal with an attractive woman. Quelle horreur, cousin, what a terrible trial. Given the circumstances, she'll be unlikely to know you for who or what you truly are and so you won't have to lie, you can simply relax and be yourself."

Julian returned the look and sighed.

The thought had its appeal, that was certain. It had been a long time since he'd been able to do even that much. The curse of money and the illusion of power.

Nico gestured and the remote computer mouse in his hand brought the large screen display above the fireplace to life.

Under normal circumstances, Julian used the screen to display the financials of his various clients in a large enough format to see from anywhere in the room, a blessing of modern technology. He liked to pace while he thought.

Now the screen displayed the familiar logo of one of the more popular internet dating sites.

Lifting an eyebrow, Julian gave Nico a sardonic look. "Really?"

Nico shrugged carelessly. "You've tried everything else, Julian. To no success."

That was true enough.

Julian had money, a great deal of it, and money changed everything. They'd both attended business occasions, society events and charity dinners, but once it was known who Julian was, the atmosphere inevitably changed. The lure of his money was simply too great.

Julian wished, suddenly and fiercely, that he could meet the one woman to whom it wouldn't matter.

"You won't meet someone like this anywhere else," Nico said.

Julian straightened a little.

The image of a lovely woman appeared on the screen, the picture clearly professionally taken.

Her hair was a rich brown with paler highlights and framed an attractive face. By the look of her, she was around thirty, perhaps a little older. Although younger women could be and were pleasant diversions, only a rare few that age bothered to know much of the world around them. That was a necessity in Julian's world. He needed someone who wouldn't just grace his arm but could also stand on her own in a room full of people with influence. She had to have confidence, even in unfamiliar circumstances, and yet he needed something else. Something more.

This woman also didn't have the polished, practiced expression of indifference that most of the women they met wore like a mask. Or that predatory look he'd seen in the faces of so many in his own circle, a coldness he couldn't like.

He glanced at Nico, who knew him well and whose tastes were almost identical to his own. That wasn't surprising considering their years together. Whether it was a matter of having been brought up together or simply an affinity they shared hardly mattered. They were much alike in many ways, including taste. And appearance. Although there were clear differences between them – Nico's eyes were more hazel than his own – many mistook them for brothers, as they were both tall, dark-haired, with strong features.

The woman on the screen did have a certain appeal. Her features were lovely, but something was missing. What it was Julian couldn't quite put a finger on. A softness in her features, in the look in her eyes. He wanted someone with strength, someone who would challenge him.

He sighed and shook his head. "No."

With a shrug, Nico said, "She was only a possibility."

He brought up the next one, but one look at her profile had them shaking their heads in astonishment, laughing.

The next few were attractive, but more importantly, Julian found he was enjoying this strange 'hunt.' He was somewhat amused by what the women said about themselves on their profiles, some by clear intention, and sometimes not. For himself, he liked humor in his women, although so far none of those he'd seen really appealed to him.

Nico gestured at the screen and clicked the mouse.

The woman displayed on the screen was a horse of a different color altogether.

Julian went still, transfixed.

"Well now," he said as he walked slowly toward the screen.

Perhaps some would have argued the point, but she was definitely attractive, her features classic, and those eyes – sharp, brilliantly blue, piercing. Her dark hair was short and a bit spiked. There was something else there, too, something in the look in her eye. Character. A touch of the hunter, a directness, a sureness and confidence many of those he'd met or they'd looked at lacked.

Smothering a grin, Nico changed pages to display the woman's profile information.

He'd done a little searching.

For a moment, Julian went still, looking at the screen, and then he burst out laughing. "How unlikely, and yet how perfect."

Slowly, letting his grin show, Nico said, "As you say, both unlikely and perfect."

Julian walked closer, taking in the image on the screen, enraptured.

"That's more like it. Much more like it. Her I would very much like to meet."

Grinning, Nico folded his arms in satisfaction, keeping his glee to himself. He might be a geek and a nerd, and not the financial and marketing guru Julian was, but he knew how to make a presentation. He'd deliberately kept this one until last. He knew Julian's tastes well, as they were a mirror to his own. She'd intrigued him. He looked at the dark-haired woman on the screen. More than intrigued him, she stirred him as well.

Julian turned to look at him. "So, how do we do this?"

Chapter Two

THE AMBASSADOR CLUB was a major step up from Rafaela's usual dates. Online matchmaking services were *so* not her, but she was getting desperate. It was difficult to find a decent man these days and even harder with her job. Given her surroundings, though, she had higher hopes this time. Unlike her last internet date, she was meeting this one in one of the most exclusive restaurants in the city. She loved the cool elegance of the room, the low-key lighting, and the flights of architectural fancy.

Arching beams soared over her head while glass panels overhead gave a view of the stars and pale sheer drapes framed the view of the lights of the city below. At the center of the room, a grand piano was surrounded by a small dance area. As the pianist played, he crooned old romantic standards. She recognized the song *Smoke Gets in Your Eyes* and smiled.

She walked into the room confidently, hoping to hide any indication of uncertainty. This also wasn't her usual environment, although she much preferred it.

The luxurious surroundings certainly didn't intimidate her, nor did the circumstances. On a day-to-day basis, she met people on both ends of the scale. She hardly cared about money. Although some considered hers a blue-collar job, it didn't mean she didn't appreciate the finer things in life. While what she did wasn't nearly as glamorous as TV portrayed it, the unpredictable hours made it difficult for her to meet people. As a result, her love life hadn't been exactly stellar lately, and her choices a bit limited.

A place like this begged the question, though – what was a man who could afford this and looked like his profile picture doing using an online matchmaking service?

Internet dating helped refine her options in many ways, except when people lied... and they lied a lot. They posted ten-year-old pictures, took off coke-bottle glasses. A few extra pounds didn't mean looking as if you were trying to smuggle a basketball under your shirt – either they were lying to themselves or in the hope their date would forgive them. How could you start any kind of relationship on a lie, though, a lie that indicated you didn't like yourself much?

Frankly, she was getting tired of it, but she was lonely and there were days when it would have been nice to have someone to come home to. Someone to play with. She was a normal woman, more or less, with a healthy, if slightly overactive, sex drive. She smiled a little at that thought.

Still, what was a girl to do? She hadn't met anyone remotely interesting any other way. It wasn't as if she met too many eligible men at work.

The usual assortment of businessmen of various heights and sizes sat around the bar. One or two looked intriguing and were probably married or gay. She wouldn't mind making a little conversation, though, if the date didn't work out. It would be nice to sit and talk to someone about politics, the weather...anything other than work.

Rafi was aware of eyes on her, of the men watching her. She wasn't uncomfortable with it, she was accustomed to it, she had the kind of body that drew stares. But some men forgot there was a person attached to that body. What was worse, though, was that it sometimes seemed as if one man wasn't enough for her. She was affectionate by nature, and that scared more than a few men off.

She made her way to the bar, sat, and ordered a drink as the pianist played As Time Goes By.

The blatantly romantic song made her smile, thinking of Rick and Elsa from Casablanca. Maybe it was an omen. She hoped so.

HEADS TURNED, CATCHING Julian's attention. He turned as well to watch the woman who entered the bar. Recognition jolted him.

She was his date.

He was more than pleased to find there were no unpleasant surprises, she was exactly as advertised. If anything, her picture hadn't done her justice. A camera couldn't quite capture her air of wry amusement. While she wasn't classically beautiful, she was lovely, her eyes sharp, curious, and a little amused. Those arresting eyes were blue, a little stormy in color, her mouth finely shaped and firm. He liked the curiosity in those eyes. Almost unconsciously, she moved in time to the music, hips swaying, a small smile playing on her lips as she walked to the bar. Her eyes sparkled, clearly pleased by the ambiance. He liked that, too. After all, it was his restaurant.

Her body?

Julian sighed with pure pleasure. That was very nice, fit but curved in all the right places, her breasts high and firm, hips rounded but tight, proportional to the rest of her. The dress was marvelous - fluid silk in a color to match those incredible eyes. It slid over her body as she walked, the neckline revealing enough of her breasts to entice without being obvious. Her legs were phenomenal, shapely, and well-muscled, with a dancer's taut calves.

According to her online profile, her tastes were as eclectic as his in everything from music to literature. That was important. He liked well-rounded women. He needed to be able to talk to someone besides Nico about things that mattered – something he found sorely lacking these days. She liked almost everything he did – most music but not the kinds he loathed – she'd read everything from the classics to fantasy. She admitted to liking romance novels, unlike those who pretended they didn't. That honesty was refreshing. She seemed open-minded as well. That was also important, he'd experienced too much to be tolerant of those whose minds were closed, plus he dealt with clients of all kinds and preferences.

Overall, he liked what he saw. Certainly, he couldn't argue too much that she drew the eyes of so many of the men here. In fact, he felt a certain amount of pride in it. After all, she was here for him.

Now, if only he liked what was inside the skin, what was behind those sharp eyes. He watched as she leaned an elbow on the bar to wait for the bartender and went to greet her.

Catching movement from the corner of her eye, Rafi turned to watch the man who walked toward her.

Now that, she thought, *is very nice*.

He was tall, around six feet or thereabouts, with a thick head of expertly styled black hair that gleamed like a raven's wing beneath the lights, deep and dark, casting off bluish highlights. It wasn't perfectly razor cut, yet on him that worked. Then there were his eyes, so dark a brown they were almost black, long-lashed and beautiful, yet there was nothing feminine about them or him. Those eyes were intelligent and aware, his gaze confident. With reason. His mouth was sensual but firm. His features were aristocratic, his cheekbones defined, his nose slightly aquiline.

But that mouth...had she mentioned she really liked his mouth?

He was undeniably handsome.

Then there was his body. She took a breath through lungs that suddenly felt constricted.

Broad shoulders moved beneath a perfectly tailored jacket. His tie had been loosened a little for comfort but was still knotted precisely.

He moved loosely, easily, and gracefully, with a touch of the predator about him. That was very promising. She thought she caught a hint of muscle concealed beneath his dress shirt. Sex seemed to pour off him, from the light in his eyes to the way he moved. She shivered a little – a touch of anticipation, of excitement. A rush of heat went through her.

What was hiding underneath that marvelously fitted shirt? she wondered.

She wouldn't have minded running her hands over that crisp material to find out. Maybe she'd get the chance.

He was walking straight toward her.

He also bore a strong resemblance to the picture of the man on the internet. For once, the picture was accurate. It seemed he really was her date. She was astonished. Her pulse picked up. She'd hit the jackpot. This promised to be very interesting.

His eyes studied her curiously, and an eyebrow lifted a fraction.

To her surprise, she found she was looking forward to the rest of the evening.

Julian wondered what amused her as her lips curved, her eyes lightening as he approached her.

Tilting her head sideways a little, she smiled and asked, "Julian Lüceanu?"

When she smiled, she went from lovely to truly beautiful in an instant. To his pleasure, his heart and breath caught a little. It had been some time since a woman had affected him so quickly.

She surprised him, too, by not mangling his last name. Another point in her favor.

Julian smiled, inclining his head a little in acknowledgment. "Then you would be Rafaela Stratford?"

Her intense blue gaze assessed him.

Rafi was accustomed to making quick appraisals of people, it was necessary in her line of work.

He was handsome, but not arrogant about it. There was pride in his stance, dignity without conceit, and strength underneath it all.

Not just physical strength, either, although she suspected he was far stronger than he appeared on the surface. On close inspection, there was definitely muscle beneath that shirt. To her astonishment, she also sensed honor and a strength of character not often seen anymore. It was something about his manner, the way he carried himself. He wasn't a man to trifle...or one to trifle with.

His voice was marvelous, just a little deep, with the faintest trace of an accent. Her heart fluttered a little.

Still...

"I would be, but my friends call me Rafi," she said, intrigued.

Lifting her hand to his lips in a courtly gesture that didn't look stupid on him at all, he gazed at her with those sexy, dark, liquid eyes.

His warm lips on her skin sent a flush of heat through her.

"So, Rafaela," Julian asked, a rush going through him at the invitation he could see in her expression, "am I to be a friend, then?"

He watched her lips twitch in response to the light brush of his lips over her knuckles.

"Oh, there's a strong possibility of that," she said, her eyes twinkling before her gaze softened at the romantic gesture.

Julian very much liked that light in her eyes.

He also liked the slender curve of her throat, the way her hair gleamed in the lights, the way she sat so straightly, so elegantly. So many American women slumped unattractively, and most didn't know how to walk properly either, clumping around in their expensive, uncomfortable designer shoes.

"Will you join me?" he asked, waiting for her assent before nodding to the maitre d'.

The man escorted them to a secluded table by the windows with the best view of the city lights below. That view was truly breathtaking, as was the man Rafi was with.

She glanced at Julian as he held her chair for her.

"Thank you, Philip," Julian said quietly, as he took his own seat.

He watched Rafaela Stratford.

Her expression softened, and her lips parted a little in pure pleasure as she looked out over the city. What surprised him was the proprietary air in her look.

So she saw the city as her own. As did he. That was intriguing.

No sooner had Rafi sat than the sommelier arrived with champagne in a bucket. A very good champagne. She looked at Julian, and one eyebrow lifted as she noted the label on the bottle.

Julian had ordered the very best, his own vintage, and was pleased by her reaction. So, she knew wines.

The sommelier poured the sparkling liquid into their glasses.

Lifting hers, Rafaela nodded and took a slow sip, rolling it around in her mouth before she sighed with pleasure at the taste.

Julian watched her eyelids flutter as she savored the wine and was heartened even more. She was both an expressive and a sensualist. Even better.

Clearly approving their selection, the sommelier departed.

The look in Rafi's eyes as her gaze met Julian's was far too wise, and he saw that mobile mouth twitch once again in amusement. She was on to him already and refused to be impressed by the show of wealth. That was a very good sign.

"Oh, I like you," he said and watched her expression turn impish, a smile brightening those brilliant, perceptive eyes.

She had a lovely and engaging smile, truly beautiful. Color touched her cheeks as she took another sip of the champagne.

Studying him from beneath her lashes, Rafi enjoyed the taste of the excellent champagne. She couldn't help but notice the effort he was making to impress her.

"I like you, too," she said, "but I have to ask, what's a man like you doing using an internet dating service?"

Lifting his own glass, he took a careful sip, his dark eyes watching her. Somehow, he made the small gesture look elegant, graceful.

"A man like me?" he said, his tone noncommittal, but his lips turned up a little as he watched her. And she watched him in return.

Rafi gave him a meaningful look, tilting her head, her eyebrow lifting, and he laughed at her knowing expression.

"Somehow, I don't think you need to fish for compliments," she said as she gestured around them, "but you're a very attractive man and wealthy enough to afford this. The kind of men I usually meet aren't the kind of men I'd want to date. But you? You could have your pick of women."

Julian smiled, shrugged negligently, and leaned back a little in his chair as he gave her request some thought. She was perceptive.

"No, I rarely need to fish for compliments," he admitted.

He looked down into the glass of champagne, swirled it idly.

"This was my cousin Nico's idea. Most of the women I meet are the wives, girlfriends, or daughters of business acquaintances and, therefore, off-limits. Or they're in the business of accumulating wealth themselves, and that's all that interests them. A more conventional service would have given me more of the same. I didn't want that. Although I've known wealth, it hasn't always been so. I find I have difficulty relating to women like that."

He stared into his glass, turned it in his fingers, glanced up at her.

Those lovely, sharp eyes were fixed on him, clearly curious. It wasn't just show. So he continued.

"Then there are those who seek wealth, wait staff, secretaries. All they wish is to enjoy the trappings of money and power. They're content to be a decoration on my arm and a companion in my bed. They gauge their responses to mine, echoing my opinions without a thought of their own. That's not enough. I want something more. I want someone I can talk to, someone who will challenge me."

So far, Rafi was that, perceptive, forthright, and honest. It made for a refreshing change.

"In what way?" she asked.

"Someone with whom I can spend a pleasant evening," he said, taking her hand before lifting it to his lips. "Someone I can talk to, have a conversation with."

Her blue eyes studied him. Assessed him.

It was something to which he wasn't quite accustomed, but he found he liked it.

He made a comment about the current political situation and she responded intelligently, with quiet heat. Points for all three, especially the intelligence and passion. That boded well too.

Passion was passion. To be passionate about anything meant there was the possibility of being passionate about other things.

He liked her quick smiles, too, the way her eyes sparkled when she talked, the way her fingertips brushed the back of his hand or his forearm when she wanted to make a point.

Rafi hadn't had the opportunity to talk to anyone like this in ages, and, although the champagne had loosened her tongue a little, it didn't concern her as sparks flew between them in more ways than one.

The conversation wandered until the piano player played the opening bars to *A Kiss to Build a Dream On*.

"Dance with me?" Julian asked, his eyes level on hers.

Rafi smiled as he stood and offered his hand.

A small curl of warmth went through her at the thought.

Taking the offered hand, she allowed him to lead her out onto the small dance floor by the piano. He swung her gracefully into his arms as the old romantic tune played. He danced beautifully, his hand firmly against her lower back, pulling her close until her hips were nestled against his. Rafi's throat tightened as his breath fluttered over her throat. A man who danced well generally made love well... and he danced very well. He'd just scored major points.

Even in heels, she was aware of her height – or lack thereof – but not in a bad way as she looked up into his face. She was more than capable of taking care of herself, but here she sensed she didn't have to.

The soft, spicy aroma of his cologne seemed to surround her, draw her closer. Rafi was incredibly conscious of his body against hers, of the strong muscles of his shoulders as they flexed beneath her hand. There was power in the body hidden beneath the business shirt and dark suit. A rush of heat went through her as his lips brushed softly against her ear. She shivered a little, closing her eyes with a sigh as her pulse quickened.

When she opened her eyes, she found he was looking at her, his dark eyes intense.

Her heart beat a little faster as his mouth lowered slowly to hers. The kiss was warm, marvelous. He tasted lightly of champagne. His lips alternately firm and soft, he explored her mouth with his tongue, tasting her as well.

The man could definitely kiss.

Breathing her in, Julian found the scent of her skin to be soft, sweet. She moved gracefully against him as they danced. Her movements were unconsciously enticing as her hips slid against his in rhythm to the music. Julian hardened pleasantly just at that. Very nice.

Carefully, he lowered his head to her throat to brush his mouth gently against it. Her pulse beat strong and rapid beneath his lips. She shivered and gasped a little.

He closed his eyes and smiled. That responsiveness was another point in her favor. He wanted a woman with passion, desire, one who wasn't afraid to show it.

And now that his mouth had found hers?

His own heart pounded in turn as her lips moved firmly beneath his. She tasted delicious, clean, beneath the crisp tang of the champagne. He loved the feel of her firm body molded against his. It was intoxicating. He'd never responded to a woman so swiftly or with such intensity before.

She pulled away a little, and he was surprised to feel a twinge of loss. It shocked him that he wanted her so much so quickly, and yet he did. After so many disappointments, he braced himself for another until he looked into her eyes. What he saw there wasn't rejection, but a question.

Deliberately, Rafi drew back, even though her body hummed in response to him. When had she felt such electricity in a simple kiss? Kissing Julian wasn't simple, though, not by a long shot. She swallowed hard, looking into his intense dark eyes. Something called to her in that steady gaze. She sensed the strength in him, a strength she could lean on.

It shook her. That was entirely unexpected.

Taking a deep breath, she looked up into his handsome, aristocratic face – evenly, squarely.

He was so beautiful, and his body felt wonderful against hers, the sheer power in it astonishing. A shot of longing, of lust, went straight to her core. And her heart.

She knew it would be easier to walk away from him now than later. Much easier. She needed to be straight with him from the beginning.

"If you're looking for a one-night stand," she said bluntly, "I'm not interested."

She'd been there, done that, and was tired of waking up in the morning alone. Some days it was difficult enough for her to get up, much less from an empty bed.

"If you're not sure you're interested in a relationship right now," she said, "come talk to me when you are. I'm not looking for promises of forever, just someday or maybe, just honesty."

Looking into her intense blue eyes, Julian almost smiled in relief. He liked and respected her directness. Her gaze on his was steady and sure, but he could also see the vulnerability she hid even from herself.

"Neither am I," he said. It was nothing more than the truth. "I want much, much more. I've had my fill of one-night stands. No promises, we'll take it one step at a time, but I can assure you of that much. And I like you, Rafaela Stratford."

He drew her gently back into his arms. She felt very good there. With one hand, he brushed the soft black hair away from her face and brought his mouth down to hers for another taste of her sweetness and spice. It was intoxicating. Already he longed for more.

If it was just for him... but it wasn't.

That was for later, hopefully. If it had been in him at that moment to pray, he would have.

One step at a time.

"Are you hungry, Raffia?" he asked softly.

The original plan had been for a late dinner, but there was clearly no need for it. What he was hungry for they didn't serve here. He tightened his arms around Rafi a little.

Rafi searched his eyes, smiling at the play on her name. If anything, it reassured her. This wasn't a game for him. Unless it was honey or babe, men didn't give nicknames to someone for whom they felt nothing. So she wasn't the only one who felt the spark that had made her stomach flutter. She was also fairly certain she couldn't have eaten a bite, not even if the most enticing steak was set in front of her.

"No," she said. "Are you?"

"A little," he admitted, "but I can wait."

Frowning slightly, Rafi said, "Are you sure?"

"Quite," he assured her. "I'm not ready for the evening to be over, but I don't know that I want to stay here. Will you walk with me a while?"

Maybe the cooler air outside would help her overheated body.

It did and it didn't.

They walked through rain-washed streets, Rafi's arm through Julian's, laughing and talking. She felt the muscle in his arm beneath the perfectly tailored suit.

He seemed to enjoy her company, bowing his head now and then to hear her replies to his comments.

Once or twice, he swung her into his arms unexpectedly to kiss her senseless. The first time he did it, it surprised her. One moment they were laughing, and the next she found herself in his arms and his lips on hers.

Unconsciously, she wrapped her hands around his strong wrists as he halted, the motion bringing her around in front of him as he brought his hands up to cup her face.

By itself, the tenderness of the gesture alone nearly undid her. She didn't get that much.

His lips touched hers with such obvious delight, such evident pleasure, she was caught off-guard in more ways than one.

For a moment, he drew back to look at her, his fingers sliding deeper into her hair. The intensity and heat in his gaze set off a firestorm inside her as his lips lowered to settle over hers once again. He took her mouth deeply with his tongue as his hands skimmed down her back to pull her closer, to mold her body against his.

Rafi slid her hands up into his dark, silky hair as his hands settled on her hips. Her body seemed to be one pulse point, throbbing and aching. It surprised her, she'd never reacted to a man so strongly, so quickly.

For the first time in a long time, Rafi felt a breath of hope.

She'd become cynical, even jaded, and she knew it. And hated it.

She found she didn't care that it was getting late. She was on the night shift starting the next evening, so it didn't matter how late she stayed out, she could sleep come morning. The more they talked the happier she was, the more they kissed, the warmer she felt.

Excitement fluttered inside her, something she hadn't felt in a very long time.

They came to a stop and Julian drew her into his arms once more, but this time the intensity and heat of his gaze nearly scorched her as he stroked a hand into her hair. He studied her face as if memorizing every line of it, seeking something in her expression, in her eyes.

He gestured, with a sigh. "My car."

Never, never, get into a vehicle with a man you don't know, her brain and training said. She ignored them.

It was a very nice Mercedes convertible, a discreet dark blue, with a soft gray leather interior that was definitely custom.

Rafi looked at him.

Taking a deep breath, Julian brushed the hair back from her face with both hands, looked into her brilliant blue eyes, and answered the question in them.

To his surprise, it was very nearly dawn. They'd walked and talked the night away, which shouldn't have been such a shock to him, but was.

"I very much want this evening to continue," he said, with a glance at the lightening sky, "but it's growing late, or rather, early, and I don't want to rush this. Can we meet again soon? Perhaps tomorrow night?"

Rafi looked at him, and there was regret in her eyes.

"I can't, I'm working midnights," she said, "but I'll be free Monday evening."

Disappointment was shockingly sharp, but her offer heartened him. It would also give him and them time to be sure.

"Monday it is, then," he said, "I'd like to show you my home, if that's all right, and introduce you to my cousin, Nico. This was his idea, after all. I think you'll like him. I know he'll like you."

She smiled. "I'd like that. I'd like that very much."

With a slight smile and a small inclination of his head, Julian said quietly, "If you'll trust me, unless you drove here, I can drive you home or we can call Uber, Lyft, or a cab."

He wanted a little more time with her, far more intensely than he'd believed possible. Now, given how intoxicated he was becoming with her, it was rapidly becoming imperative. Most of the women he met were far too aware of his wealth. Rafi seemed not to care about anything except Julian Lüceanu, the man. Her glance at his car had shown that, appreciation for a finely crafted machine had been evident, but that was all the notice she gave to it.

More though, was the feel of her mouth against his, her sweet body so pliant. They fired his blood and made him hunger for her in a way he'd never hungered for anyone.

If it were only him, there would be no question.

He wanted it to be tonight. He wanted it to be now, but he wouldn't – couldn't – rush either of them.

With a smile, she nodded. She'd taken a taxi rather than riding her motorcycle. Bikes and dresses didn't mix well.

What would his home be like? Rafi wondered, curiosity tugging at her. "That would be wonderful."

Opening the car door, he offered her his hand.

She smiled.

The Mercedes was even more comfortable than she'd expected. He drove it competently and just a little fast.

To her surprise, he walked her to her door, an old-fashioned courtesy she found charming.

It wasn't often she was charmed.

He lowered his mouth to hers, brushed his lips lightly over hers, teasingly, before he allowed them to settle.

Heat rushed through her as he drew her close and took the kiss deeper.

Rafi was intensely aware of his powerful body pressed against hers, of the strength of the arms that banded around her.

"Something to remember me by," he said, his deep voice seeming to echo inside her.

She wasn't likely to forget. He had classic, old-world manners, a Mercedes, and very expensive tastes in champagne.

Far more importantly, she'd enjoyed his company tremendously. She liked the warmth, the desire in his eyes.

She wished the night wasn't over. Already she anticipated seeing him again.

Monday couldn't come too soon.

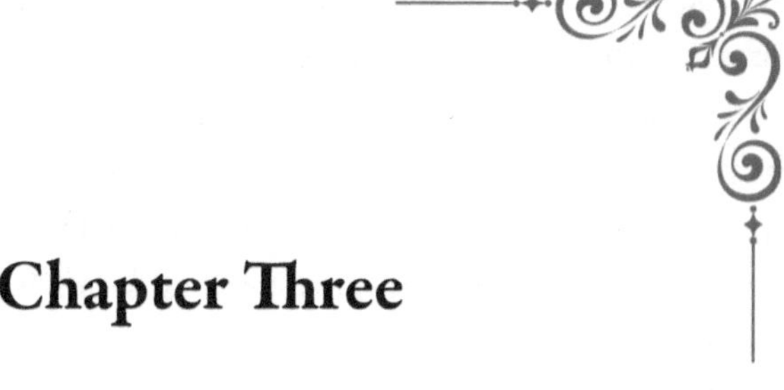

Chapter Three

BEYOND RAFI'S DESK was another world. Not one she minded. Going over files and filling in reports, Rafi watched the parade pass by before her. Unlike what they showed on TV there was little that was romantic about what she saw. No glass walls separated detectives from perpetrators. Glass would have incredibly stupid when objects and people were likely to go flying, although that didn't happen as often as it did on TV either. There was no fancy lighting, just fluorescent tubes that flickered enough to give you a headache.

She and her partner Sasha had the midnight shift this week so unless somebody popped someone in a bar fight or a domestic, or either boiled over into more than a punching match, they were pretty much desk-bound, bringing old cases up to speed. Ninety-nine percent boredom offset by one percent adrenaline when they did have to respond to a call. At that hour they couldn't even talk to witnesses in their current caseload unless they wanted to roust a hooker or question a bartender.

Of course, there was also the increasing chance that some of the newly free paranormals would act up.

Like every 'immigrant' group, there were layers. Now that they didn't have to hide, it hadn't taken long for some of the younger and poorer to separate out into gangs of anything from packs of werewolves to mixed groups of shapeshifters and vampires, as testosterone-filled as their more 'normal' counterparts.

Some of those gangs had morphed into something far more, prostitution and dealing drugs, as had the immigrants before them.

It had been inevitable ever since the first paranormal revealed himself to be a werewolf who'd found it increasingly impossible in more modern times to conceal what he was. Once he'd outed himself, had broken that barrier, paranormals of all kinds had suddenly come out of the 'closet' as it were.

With them had come an entirely new set of problems – nutcases of all kinds, with all their prejudices and preconceptions, especially the religious fanatics.

Several people had been injured before they discovered that despite the movies silver didn't make good bullets, which spoke well of the restraint of the paranormals involved.

A number of arrests were made after threats against paranormals became public. Searches of perps revealed everything from stakes, mallets, and various items of soft metals – gold and silver primarily – to stolen holy water. Rafi would have thought that stealing holy water would pretty much invalidate it, but maybe that was just her.

It was no wonder many paranormals stayed hidden.

Sometimes Rafi wished human beings didn't find so many ways to separate themselves, so many reasons to hate and kill each other. But then she'd be out of a job.

Rafi sighed at the thought and turned back to her paperwork.

"So," Sasha said, "I forgot to ask, how'd the date go?"

Looking up Rafi smiled at the memory and at her partner.

Sasha was a big, good-looking guy with a lean handsome face and warm brown eyes. He was the best partner she'd ever had. The rest of the squad often joked that they were the long and short of it, given her diminutive size, or that she was the brains while he was the brawn although he was easily as smart as she was and just as good a cop. Not to mention she could kick most of their asses. Affection ran deep between them, but that was as far as it went. Neither had ever felt the slightest spark of attraction and neither would have changed a thing about their relationship. Their friendship was just too good for that.

"It went...good."

Sasha lifted an eyebrow at her as he looked up from his paperwork.

"With that grin," he said, "it seems like it was probably better than good."

Rafi shook her head wryly. "It was only one date, Sash."

She was trying desperately not to make too much about it, but the hours between now and Monday seemed to be passing far too slowly.

He gave her another look, knowing her too well.

"Okay, so it went good, really good," she admitted. "It was a really good date."

If Rafi had one true friend in the world, it was Sasha. They'd been through a lot since they'd been partnered three years previously. Trust was essential between partners and he'd trusted her with his deepest secret. Not that he'd had much choice.

Sasha was a werewolf.

According to regs, Sasha wasn't even really supposed to be on the police force any more than any other paranormal. His greater strength and speed were considered unfair to the general public and a werewolf's supposedly chancy temper was a danger, a liability that opened the PD up to lawsuits if someone got hurt, or Sasha lost control.

It wasn't fair, especially considering the danger those on the job faced going up against paranormals, but that was the way it was. A few fought it through the courts while others just kept quiet about what they were.

Like Sasha.

He was a great cop, though, and in the years they'd known each other he'd never once lost control in Rafi's presence. He had his other nature locked down pretty tight. If he had any questions about it, or on nights when the moon was close and full and he wasn't sure of himself, he locked himself in a room in the basement of his house. That didn't happen often.

She'd never seen him change and didn't want to. It wasn't that it turned her off or anything, it was just...private. She respected that.

Like her date.

Rafi shook her head. Some things she couldn't say even to Sasha.

Like that the evening had seemed almost magical.

Thoughts like that just weren't her nature.

It was so weird.

"I've never connected to someone so quickly," she blurted, almost abashed. "I met him at the Ambassador Club."

Sasha's eyebrows shot up. "That's high-end."

"I know," she said. "So is he. Tailored suit and all."

Warmth washed through her at the memory of Julian as he'd walked toward her. Her little heart had gone pitter pat at the sight of him. It still did at the memory.

"Wow," Sasha said with a grin. "I'm impressed. He certainly seems to be going all out. So, when are you going to see him again?"

"Monday," she said.

At the memory of Julian's mouth on hers her heart did more than pitter pat and more than warmth washed through her.

Sasha folded his hands on their shared desk and looked at her. "Have you told him you're a cop?"

Taking a breath, Rafi shook her head, looked down at her desk. "No, not yet."

His tone gentle, Sasha said, "Why not?"

She looked up at him. He knew why not. All the baggage, the expectations.

"I want him to get to know me first. Me. Not the cop."

"Yeah, I know, Rafi," he said and sighed. "But you have to tell him."

She knew that. She did.

"Monday. I'll tell him Monday."

BLOOD BOUND

When she went to see his house, to meet his cousin.
It couldn't come soon enough.

Chapter Four

RAFI ADMIRED THE SCENERY as it passed, intrigued and amused as Julian drove through what seemed like mile after mile of vineyards that spread out on each side of the drive. A pergola ran along both sides of the road. At least a mile of it. The supports were twined with wisteria and clematis in every color of the rainbow. All of it lit by the warm glow of the setting sun.

Then the vineyards gave way to a broad expanse of neatly clipped green lawn and at last she could see Julian's house.

Except it wasn't a house, it was a mansion.

The driveway was a sweep of intricately set pavers that must have cost a fortune, and not a small one, to set in place. The garage housed several high-end cars, the building itself larger than most people's houses. Including her own apartment.

Julian brought the car to a stop and handed her out of the car as she looked around.

Broad marble steps led up to a wide slate patio shaded by a central oak.

Built of stone, the house itself resembled a small castle.

Planters of Japanese maples and flowering bushes flanked the doorways, the lighting soft and indirect. More light glowed warmly through what appeared to be real leaded-glass windows. Through one set Rafi could see a library filled with aged, leather-bound books.

The main doorway itself was grand, an intricate filigree of wrought iron over ancient carved oak.

She glanced at Julian and lifted an eyebrow.

With a small shrug, he said, "I might have a little bit of spare change here and there."

His dark eyes twinkled with mischief.

She looked at him, smiled, and shook her head.

"A little spare change?" she said. "In addition to the Mercedes, there's a Jag, a Maserati and a Land Rover in the garage."

Julian shrugged. "True."

"All right," she said, laughing, "I'll admit it. I'm impressed."

Impressed, but not overawed. She wasn't a woman who impressed easily. Julian liked that.

Grinning, he said, his hand at the small of her back, "Good. I was hoping."

That made her laugh again. He liked that about her, her easy laughter.

He opened the door to the house for her.

"Shouldn't you have servants for this? A butler or something?" she asked with a wave of her hand, giving him a teasing look from beneath her lashes as he escorted her into the foyer.

Her gaze was appreciative as she looked around the entry, taking in the thick Persian carpet on the floor and the antique table with the flower arrangement centered on it. Real, fresh flowers, the scent of which filled the room.

Much entertained, he said, "I gave him and them the night off."

She looked back at him and raised an eyebrow as she said, "Did you now? Anticipating, were you?"

Oh, she was quick.

A hint of challenge lit her eyes.

Julian let his hand slide down to the small of her back once again to guide her into the library, enjoying the contact even as he tried not to let his nervousness show. He hoped she was the woman he thought she was. He liked the look of her in his home.

Mahogany hair gleamed in the light as she glanced back at him, blue eyes twinkling intriguingly, her lips curving.

She fit. She was a work of art in herself, a fine sculpture wrought of ivory and expensive wood.

That look alone was fascinating, engaging.

Her heels tapped lightly on the intricately tiled mosaic of the entryway before the carpet in the library muffled the sound.

"Let's say I was hopeful," he said, smiling in return, enjoying the banter despite his tension as they walked from the foyer into the library.

The room was impressive, with brocade draperies and dark wooden furniture that was clearly antique. Ancient tapestries decorated the walls between the bookcases. Art deco lamps illuminated the room, slender feminine figures reaching upward gracefully. A large screen was set above the fireplace. Despite the eclectic mix of styles and eras, it all worked somehow. It was lush, plush, and appeared surprisingly comfortable.

A laugh rang out, startling them both. "Oh, I do like her, Julian. She'll do very well."

Rafi turned, to find they weren't alone.

Holding up a hand, Julian said, "Raffia, don't be alarmed. As I told you, I wanted to introduce you to my cousin, Nico. Nico, this is Rafi."

Rafi glanced at Julian and then looked at his cousin.

A glass of golden liquid, too dark to be a white wine in his hand, Nico stood at the back of the room. He eyed her with evident curiosity, his head tilted slightly.

Leaner than Julian, Nico's eyes were more almond-shaped, a long-lashed golden brown instead of Julian's depthless black. As aristocratic as his cousin in looks and bearing, Nico's features were a little broader, not quite as fine or aquiline.

Where Julian was exotically and finely handsome, Nico was more down-to-earth.

"Would you like some wine?" Nico asked, as he held up his glass to admire it in the light. "Or something stronger, perhaps? Please not a puerile Chablis or Chardonnay."

There was something in his voice, a bit of a dare.

Rafi remembered the vineyards that stretched out on both sides of the long driveway. A Chablis or Chardonnay would be a safe choice and one most women would take, appropriate for dinner or sitting on the terrace but not for a slightly cool evening.

"I would, please," she said, giving him a look of amusement as she glanced from him to Julian. "If what you're having is a sherry or something just as rich but not too sweet, I'd like some of it, please."

His eyes glinting in return, Nico bowed his head a little.

Judging by that look, she'd passed his test.

Julian took her hand and raised it to his lips, smiling. "One for me as well, Nico, if you don't mind?"

Rafi smiled back at him. Her pulse fluttered at the approving look in both their eyes.

Dressed more casually than Julian in jeans, a white shirt, and long bare feet, Nico crossed the floor toward them, two glasses of golden fortified wine in his free hand.

Where Julian moved deliberately, Nico stalked like a tiger and yet Rafi sensed no real threat from him. For all his sardonic air, she sensed kindness in him, a warmth he carefully hid.

She'd known more than a few men like him, more sensitive in nature than they wanted to appear. The ironic tone of his voice was nothing more than a defense mechanism. That vulnerability appealed to her, it brought out her protective instincts.

Nico handed her one glass and bowed with a little smile. His fingers brushed hers as he did, lingering for just fraction of a second too long, his golden-brown eyes slanting toward her.

She sipped at the sherry as he walked behind her, warmth from it filling her. The taste was marvelous, and the warmth of it filled her.

He leaned a little close to breathe in her scent as he went past. The curiously intimate gesture somehow made her as intensely aware of him as she was of Julian.

BOTH WERE INCREDIBLY handsome, very attractive, men and her body reacted to them naturally.

For a moment, she indulged in brief erotic daydream, one that had her areole pebbling and her pussy dampening. Her own private fantasy – both men making love to her, Julian with his lovely mouth on her throat while Nico ran his tongue lightly around her bared nipple. In an instant she was hot and aching, but careful not to show it.

The sherry was very good, rich, the warming her to her toes. That didn't help.

Rafi waved a hand at the walls, looking at Julian and his cousin. Outside of a library, bookstore, or the piles scattered around her own house, she'd never seen so many books.

"Have you read all these?"

His expression softening, Julian eyed the bookshelves with evident satisfaction as he sipped his wine.

"Most, yes," he said, and then smiled wryly. "All but the computer books, those are Nico's. To me they're incomprehensible."

Nico grinned, as mischievous as a boy when he looked at Rafi. "He's a complete noob. He feels the same about texting."

The mischief in his eyes made resisting his smile impossible.

Unfortunately, she couldn't help but be aware of an undercurrent in the air. It was something about the way the two men kept glancing at each other. A silent communication. She sensed a strange tension, an invisible elephant in the room. As a cop, she had to be good at reading the signs that passed between people, the language of glances, the turn of the body. It was what she did. There was an air of...calculation...about the whole thing. Not that it bothered her much, since neither seemed threatening and she rarely went on a date unprepared.

Looking from one handsome man to the other, Rafi said, "All right, do you want to tell me what this is really all about?"

Calmly, Rafi sipped from her glass of wine and lifted an eyebrow, trying not to notice how her heart twisted at the possibility of disappointment.

Nico burst out laughing as Julian looked from one to the other of them, clearly nonplussed.

"She has you pegged already, cousin," Nico said, amused, as he leaned back against a table.

Shooting Nico a warning look, Julian looked at Rafi intently. It wasn't funny, not really.

"I want you to know I liked you from almost the moment we met and that this is very much about you, Rafi, the person," he said. "About finding the right match. I, we, would very much like that person to be you."

He looked at Nico, who nodded, a simple incline of his head.

Julian took a breath. This would be the difficult part.

He did indeed like Rafi very much. She was mercurial, able to go from serious to laughing in the blink of an eye, she was sharp, edgy and beautiful. He liked her, but he wanted more. Much more. They both did.

"We have a proposition," he said carefully, trying to find the right words. He didn't want to lose her before they'd begun. "A personal, not business, proposition."

They'd tried something like this before and learned from experience that they needed the right person. Finding her, finding that right person, had proven far more difficult.

His – their – wealth was a powerful but short-lived aphrodisiac. Neither needed to work, save for the challenge their jobs provided them. Money, however, was cold companionship as those who loved it rarely loved anything, or anyone, else.

It had been painful each time and harder on Nico than it had been on him, as Nico had never known any other life than this one. Unlike Julian. It was an experience neither of them wished to repeat.

Rafi's eyes were still, watchful, waiting as she looked at them. Her gaze moved from one of them to the other.

It gave him hope that she seemed so unimpressed by it all. This next though, was the hard part.

There was no way to sugarcoat what he needed to say. In the past he'd tried euphemisms, had tried to approach it obliquely. None of it had worked.

Julian took a deep breath, looked into her deep blue eyes. And took a leap of faith.

Listening, watching him, seeing the earnestness and the care with which Julian was taking in choosing the right words, Rafi sighed. That wasn't a good sign. Her heart twisted a little more.

Propositions weren't so bad, though. Maybe. Especially personal ones.

First, she would hear what it was they had to say. She liked Julian, and Nico, too. Perhaps more than she should on such short acquaintance. There had been that sense of instant connection between her and Julian that first night. Something that made her heart yearn and her body ache.

She felt the same about Nico, his diffidence oddly charming.

"All right," she said, keeping her heart and head still for a moment, seeing the need in Julian's eyes. "I'm listening. Try me."

"Rafi," Julian said bluntly, "we're vampires."

There was a long, long, silence as she took it in.

Vampires. Paranormals.

Well, that explained a lot.

She looked at them, considering it.

In her job at one time or another she'd seen it all - the nutcases, the wannabes, the Goths and such. The posers and the real deal. The ones who not only walked the walk but talked the talk. Vampires, werewolves, shapeshifters of all kinds, zombies, voodoo, all of it.

There were fakes, of course.

It still surprised her how many people wanted to be paranormal, especially considering the number of paranormals who wanted to be normal. And some who were normal who wanted to be paranormal and yet were unable to make the final commitment to the change. And the ones who did. Not to mention all the paranormals who didn't want to add to their numbers for whatever reason.

As a result, there were parts of the city even cops stayed out of at certain hours or on certain nights, like the full moon. No one spoke of it, it was just understood.

Except for her and Sasha.

Walk into any convenience store or bar past a certain hour on certain days and you couldn't be sure who or what you'd run into. They'd answered calls in vampire bars where the music was loud, the clientele were Goth and younger vampires mixed with humans. Sometimes it was hard to tell one from the other. There was a strong aftermarket in 'fangs'. Some dentists actually specialized in them. It was strange to walk into one of the clubs and watch the couples in the shadowed corners, one feeding from the other, the ecstasy on both their faces astonishingly erotic.

It had felt oddly voyeuristic. And a little exciting.

You quickly learned which were real and which weren't.

Julian and Nico were very real.

Just the idea of it had her a little hot and damp between the thighs. The mental image of Julian's mouth poised at her throat now had a new meaning. A meaning that had her pussy aching more than a little. Not that she let it show.

Rafi studied them, her senses on alert. She relied on instinct and it was usually dependable. Very dependable. She was proof positive of it. She'd ventured more than once into that uncharted territory and she was still alive to talk about it.

Vampires. Both of them. Two very attractive, very handsome men.

She wasn't a complete idiot, she'd done her homework before she met Julian this second time. Just the facts. Enough to assure her he wasn't a danger to himself or others. There'd been nothing to alarm her. Not even a rumor he was a vampire. Which meant he was very, very good, and very careful.

Thoughtfully, she took a breath and looked from Julian to Nico, an eyebrow lifted doubtfully. It should be easy enough for them to prove.

With a small shrug and a sigh, Julian smiled a little uncomfortably and let a touch of his hunger show.

Rafi saw pain in his eyes. Her heart twisted a little.

She watched as his canine teeth slowly lengthened. No dentist could fake that.

Turning her head, she looked at Nico, who shrugged diffidently and smiled faintly even as his own teeth lengthened.

It was the shrugs and sighs that reassured her. That and the look in their eyes – the obvious pain in Julian's, the resignation in Nico's. Neither leaped to devour her. Her instincts were fast enough to have pulled the gun from her purse and shot one or the other of them.

Although, to her surprise, she found what they offered wasn't such a bad proposition, coming from these two very handsome men. In fact, a small thread of warmth went through her at the idea, a trickle of excitement.

She certainly didn't feel threatened.

If Julian had wanted to harm her, he'd had ample opportunity on their long walk through the deserted streets or they both could have attacked her as she walked in the door.

They hadn't.

It would have been a lot easier than this.

Whatever it was they wanted must require her consent.

"All right," she said, slowly, "so, what does this have to do with me?"

Nico looked at her and laughed. "I think we chose well, cousin."

"Not until you tell me what's going on," Rafi said, looking at him sharply. "And what it is you want from me."

Because it hurt. She'd hoped for, had wanted, more.

Somehow, though, she suspected she knew, had known from the instant she'd heard Nico's voice and seen him standing at the back of the room. A strange thrill shivered through her.

That was a secret fantasy, one she'd never told to anyone.

There was some fear too. She was used to that in her line of work, though.

What surprised her was the rush of anticipation that went through her at the idea.

She reached into her bag, withdrew her badge and holstered weapon and laid both on the table. Her gun in easy reach.

"You should know I'm a cop," she said.

Julian's dark eyes fixed on her.

"You knew," she said.

He shrugged without apology. "I'm a wealthy man, Raffia. Of course, I checked up on you."

But he liked her forthright nature and honesty as well as that indefinable air of a competent, capable woman more than able to take care of herself.

In his position Rafi could have, would have, done the same and had.

"It's nothing like that, Rafi," Julian said. "It's simple, really. Neither of us particularly care to announce we're vampires. It's no one's business but our own. And, despite the 'tolerance' our people enjoy these days, there are still misconceptions. Even so, some have become...aware."

He stared into the wine in his glass, swirled it. "It's also become a bit more dangerous. Acceptance hasn't come from all. Some still hate us for what we are. The easiest way to find us is through those from whom we feed. It's difficult these days, dangerous even, to find someone who is...willing. Many think they would be until the moment arrives. Fewer women than you'd think would actually consider it. We can compel...but to force another's will? That makes us no better than men who drug women's drinks, it's no better than rape."

For centuries he'd fought such men, he wouldn't become one.

She watched Julian's jaw tighten, his dark gaze harden. She wouldn't care to get on his wrong side, not on that issue.

"It's also not as...satisfying, and, for what we want, useless. How would we ever know if you cared for us for ourselves? That is, if you ever forgave us for the doing of it."

Given she was a cop, she wouldn't. It was a relief to know how adamant he was about it, though.

But the idea that he wanted what was between them to matter... She took a breath. That was a different thing entirely. For a moment, she wasn't a cop, she was a woman and breathless.

"What we want is a companion. Someone who's easy to get along with, whose company we enjoy. Caring is important. We want someone we feel something for, a friend, and with luck, much more. If you agree, you could come here to live with us. You'd want for nothing. If you like, we could even try it for a time, to see if you like the arrangement."

We.

Both of them. It took a minute for that to sink in.

A shiver went through her.

Once more that very private fantasy whispered in the back of her mind, sending a shimmer of heat through her. She'd never dreamed it was possible.

She looked at him, at them, getting an inkling of what he – they – wanted.

Her throat tightened a little, Julian's reserve revealing. That hadn't been her impression of him. From the first, she'd sensed he was a strong, proud man.

"I wanted to speak to you about it now," Julian said, "before emotions become too involved and someone is hurt."

His own emotions as well as Nico's and Rafi's.

There had been so much promise in their evening together. Even now, after so short a time the thought of losing her pained him. He remembered the feel of her mouth beneath his, her limber body pressed against his. How much worse would it hurt, though, if he waited until emotions were more deeply involved? Theirs as well as hers.

Hunger didn't help.

He'd scented her earlier arousal as Nico teased her verbally, heard her heartbeat increase through his enhanced senses. She wanted them, too. Not just him, but Nico as well. That was important.

Unconsciously, Julian licked his lips, ran his tongue over his teeth. He took a breath and forced his hunger back. He wasn't some ravening beast, he was a vampire, the oldest among those here in this city. That had meaning among his kind. His hunger didn't – wouldn't – rule him. If necessary, he and they could subsist on the blood of animals and had. But it was subsistence...at most, a barren existence. Craving moved within him, but he was the master, not the servant.

Walking toward them, Nico added, "Julian has a theory."

"And that theory is?" Rafi prompted, watching both carefully.

Julian fought back the esurience the faint scent the flash of her fear raised, bowing his head in the struggle, his jaw tight.

On some level Rafi knew they were both predators and responded according to her nature. Adrenaline surged, prepared her to fight or flee. Knowing it would be the former, not the latter.

Julian looked to Nico, who also struggled with his hunger.

This was the part of what he was, who they were, that Julian hated, this dependence. He'd watched the centuries pass with fascination and wonder, had known and loved many and been loved by some few. As had Nico – his beloved cousin, his friend – the one who'd stood by him all these years.

Something had been missing, always. A companion, a lover. A true mate. Someone who accepted them both for who and what they were. It was too much to expect, but still, Julian wanted it. As did Nico.

"Fear...can be like a spice," Julian said. "But pleasure is so much more so. It's... intoxicating... richer...far more satisfying. Fear is as empty as a wine bottle once it's drunk. Pleasure is so much more."

Just the thought was enough to trigger his need. Hunger burned in him.

Forcing it back, Julian took a breath. "We can visit women in their sleep, they welcome us then, but it's...unsatisfying. There are others...the homeless, but..."

He sighed.

"There are the drugs, the alcohol, which fills the blood of those desperate people. The diseases many carry have no effect on our kind, but the blood we take does have an effect on them. Even worse, though, to prey on those so helpless, so lost..."

Julian met Raffia's eyes, his expression grim. "It's not the same."

Rafi was very aware of Nico crossing behind her.

His steps slowed. Once more he stopped to breathe in her scent, his face close enough to brush her hair. A small thrill rushed through her. She looked from one to the other of them, seeing the tension in them, seeing their fangs drop. She was all too aware they were predators right now and struggling with it.

Running wouldn't help. Running would make her prey. And there was no need. Some fear was there, but she controlled it as she looked at them, knowing they wouldn't harm her unless she triggered their hunting instincts. It was hardly the first time she'd faced down a hungry predator.

And they were both very hungry.

"You're starving," she said incredulously.

With a sigh and a shrug, Julian nodded. "Not completely by any long stretch, but close enough to make the need uncomfortable."

She looked at Nico, whose levity had vanished.

He nodded as well.

"And the theory?" she asked, more than a little curious.

She found herself trying not to think of the sensation of Julian's body against hers when he'd kissed her or when his mouth had brushed over her throat. Heat moved through her nonetheless.

He'd loosened his tie and taken off his suit jacket to toss it carelessly over the back of a chair. It was easy to see now what the jacket had hidden. The pressed white cotton shirt couldn't hide the power in his chest, in his body.

The thought of that strong body pressed against hers, of his mouth closing over her throat, his teeth sinking into her...piercing her...

A shocking jolt of heat raced through her, arrowing to her core.

With an effort, she tried not to look at Nico. Tried not to think of his long, lean body against her, too.

As attracted as she was to Julian, she felt a different, equal, but very strong attraction to Nico. A fantasy she'd carried around for years. Only here she didn't have to deny it, or refuse to act on it, unless that was what she chose. Her deepest, darkest fantasies might be coming true. It seemed as if her body had turned electric as raw energy coursed through her.

"Pleasure is infinitely more satisfying than fear," Julian continued, his deep voice dropping seductively. "Better than adoration or other less...savory...excitements. Love, affection, those emotions make everything richer."

Keeping still, Rafi looked from one man to another, a thrill going through her at the implications of what was being said.

"The difficulty for us," Julian said, his eyes lowered, "is that while we enjoy the experience, we can't have both. We can feed but the moment we do..."

"We can't fuck," Nico said, bluntly. "The blood goes one place or another. It can't come in and go south at the same time."

Rafi blinked. She let out a long, slow breath. That *was* a dilemma.

"What about the whole 'changing into a vampire' thing?" she asked half curiously, surprised to find she was more than considering it. Her pulse beat heavily.

Julian swung around to look at her in disbelief.

She was thinking about it or she wouldn't have asked. And she hadn't run.

Yet.

Perhaps there was still hope.

He didn't dare allow himself so much.

"A myth," he said, "although thanks to the movies some still believe it and hunt us because of it. It takes more than one bite, it's complex. Vampire hunters, though, have a much easier job of it today, with the help of the internet. There have been threats. Rumors among our people. Yet another reason why it's better and safer for us to have a single source. They can't find us as easily."

He sighed.

It had become an increasing problem with the resurgence of fundamentalism around the globe.

Over the centuries he'd found such things went in cycles. Unfortunately, that didn't make those periods any less dangerous. There had been a woman recently among those they'd tried who'd had second thoughts come morning. Yet another who suddenly discovered once he'd fed that she still believed the myths. Julian was increasingly unwilling as time went by to take such chances with either Nico's life or his own.

In the end though, none of it mattered. The truth was they were lonely. They wanted someone to share their lives.

It ached in him as he knew it ached in Nico.

Once they'd tried to separate, but found they'd missed each other's companionship too greatly.

A solitary vampire was also vulnerable – another lesson the centuries had taught them.

Julian glanced at Nico, remembering the small, newly orphaned boy who'd been put into his care so many centuries before. Something the teenaged Julian had taken very seriously. Both Nico's parents – Nico's mother had been Julian's mother's sister – had been slaughtered in one of the many conflicts that had ravaged their homeland.

Nico had tried so hard to be brave. He'd been so young.

Times had been harsh even among the lesser nobility and so Julian had had to share his food and bed with the younger boy. Not that he'd minded much. The younger Nico had hero-worshiped his older cousin, very flattering to a fourteen-year-old taking up his first real sword.

When it had come time for Julian to choose a squire there had never been any question who it would be.

In all the years since, Nico had stood at his back, as Julian had stood at his.

With a gesture, Julian said, "The bit about drinking a vampire's blood to make the change? That works, just not immediately. It simply...preserves you...until you die truly."

So it had been for both of them when they'd changed. He and Nico had been brought over by their Queen, now many centuries dead, slaughtered when the castle had been finally overrun by their enemies. She'd died fighting. If not in appearance, in many other ways Rafi reminded Julian of his first Lady. She, too, was a warrior.

"Oddly," he said, "it's much like a virus in the blood, spread by saliva and ejaculation."

That had been one of the advantages of the new reality, of modern science.

Julian had spent a considerable amount of money investigating homo vampiris, to know exactly how they worked. The real truth was that they were just another offshoot of humanity. Not that it made a difference to some. The lies persisted, as oft-repeated lies did, particularly so long as they served another's need.

Still.

Julian lifted an eyebrow.

"As for the stories? That we could only move about at night? Nonsense. If that were true most of us would have been eradicated early. How long would it have taken for the neighbors to notice you only came out after dark? Our needs though were different from theirs and there were those who feared us, so we only hunted under the cover of darkness. Imagine how many of us there would be, though, if vampires were created the way most think, given the number of people any vampire must bite to feed? There'd be thousands of us, millions."

"And realistically," Nico added, rolling his eyes dramatically, "the human body contains about seven quarts of blood, give or take. How many people can drink a full quart in one sitting? So one vampire couldn't possibly drink a person dry, no matter what the novels suggest."

There was that, Rafi thought, grinning. Do the math. Half the world would be vampire. Or more.

Reborn at twenty-seven. There was something to be said for that.

"Pleasure though," Julian said slowly, obviously encouraged by her quick grin, "can satisfy us for a long time. You would have two men devoted to you, to your every need."

His bottomless deep brown eyes fixed on her and her breath caught.

Now she knew for certain what it was he offered.

Both of them.

She stared at him in disbelief, her eyes widening as her breath escaped her once more.

That fantasy whispered in the back of her mind.

"Imagine it," Julian said softly, sensing her capitulation, sensing her need, her desire, his voice barely a whisper, seductive, enticing. "One of us making love to you, touching you, pleasuring you until you tremble helplessly in our arms. We can intensify the experience, make it even more pleasurable than you can imagine."

The very thought sent a rush through her.

She repressed a shiver...of exhilaration? Fear? Or anticipation?

Nico interjected, "Julian believes that if we both feed from you, carefully at first, eventually your body will adjust so you can feed us both easily."

Rafi looked from one to the other of them, keeping her purse and therefore her weapon, close.

Still, she wasn't really frightened. More...excited.

Her panties were damp and her heart pounded.

Both of them.

It would be easier to keep a clear head if they weren't so damn good-looking, but her hormones raged just at the sight of them. Her hands remembered all too well the feel of the muscles of Julian's back beneath them as he kissed her. She wondered what the difference would be between Julian and Nico.

It was difficult to keep her thoughts straight. Caution warred with desire. Or was it the other way around?

"So," Rafi said, frowning a little, incredulous. She felt oddly breathless. "Let's see if I've got this right. I get to have two handsome men making love to me and in return you drink my blood? I have both of you for company, this beautiful house to live in and I want for nothing?"

They looked at her.

Julian smiled wryly. "Something like that."

She grinned back.

"Is my immortal soul at risk?" she asked lightly, only half-joking.

With that kind of deal, it had to be. Talk about too good to be true.

To her surprise, she realized she was considering it.

Both of them. Taking her.

The thought sent a burst of warmth through her, looking at the way Julian's tailored shirt fit his body, his slacks fit his narrow waist. She fought not to look at Nico, at his leaner frame, and tried not to think of what his body would feel like pressed against her. Something about his diffidence appealed to her, there was a sweetness to him that he took pains to hide while Julian's strength drew her in a completely different way.

Both of them.

Her body tightened, heated, at the thought as her gaze met Julian's and then Nico's.

Julian laughed at her wry tone and the lightness in it.

Relief swept through him in a rush even as he scented her rising arousal, her desire. He felt a breath of hope.

"A myth also, although there are some who believe it as well."

As he knew all too well from the past. Just the fact that she asked, though, meant she was considering it. For the first time in nearly a millennia, something within Julian eased. He felt hope, genuine hope for something real, something that would last.

He bowed his head in gratitude. "Raffia..."

He looked at her and then Nico, who after all the long centuries was far more than a cousin to him, more than a friend and more than a companion. As hard as it had been at times, it had been harder on Nico, who'd never been comfortable in that kind of hunt. The shallowness had worn on him as it had on Julian. They wanted more than a string of short, empty, relationships.

Both were one-woman men and it had become clear over time that only one woman would do. For both of them. One who would, could, love them both.

Finding her had been the difficulty.

Until now.

Perhaps.

Rafi thought of the endearment – Raffia – that play on her name that Julian had used at the bar.

It touched her for some reason.

Following his gaze, she turned her head to find Nico standing beside her, his golden-brown eyes brilliant.

Gently, Rafi said, in the same tone Julian had used, "Julian, I haven't said yes yet."

Was she really considering it?

To her astonishment it seemed she was. The thought had her surprisingly hot and wet, not that she let it show. After all it wasn't as if she were some fluttering virginal teenager, she was a grown woman. It was hardly the first time she'd had sex, if never with two men at once, whatever her private fantasies. Her nipples grew tight.

A thrill went through her at the very idea.

It wasn't as if she had to worry about the usual. As Julian had said, vampires were immune to human diseases.

Julian laid his hands on her shoulders, stared into her eyes steadily, reassuringly, as Nico joined them.

"Nothing will happen here that you don't want," Julian said, his gaze fixed on her.

Those intense dark eyes drew her.

He was such a beautiful man.

He brushed her hair back from her face, drew her into his arms.

Another strong arm slid around her waist from behind, to hold her tightly against a lean, hard, male body.

Nico.

They sandwiched her between them as Nico drew her hair away from her neck to run his lips lightly down the column of her throat.

A rush of heat raced through her.

There was something even more erotic about Julian watching as Nico did it.

Julian's eyes were intent on hers as Rafi shivered lightly at the sensation of Nico's mouth on her skin. Julian lowered his lips to hers and took her mouth gently, then more possessively, his tongue sweeping inside to explore as Nico nuzzled her throat.

"There are benefits," Julian said, softly, as he lifted his head to kiss her softly just beside her eye.

"More than this?" she gasped on a half laugh, and then shivered as his lips touched her ear.

He chuckled, the sound low and deep.

Rafi's body jolted, her nipples going hard.

"Yes," Julian said softly as his lips wandering down her throat on one side, while Nico pressed his mouth at the curve of her shoulder and neck on the other.

Goosebumps raced over Rafi's skin.

"Your metabolism will increase, and your endurance, you'll be more resistant to disease."

"Hmmm," Rafi said, only half hearing his words as both Julian and Nico nibbled at her throat.

Pressed between them, Rafi was very aware of the state of their arousal. It was impossible not to feel the hard ridge of Julian's cock against her belly or Nico's nestled between the cheeks of her ass and the small of her back.

She fought a moan as passion and need curled deep in her belly, fired her blood, and made her pussy ache.

Almost reluctantly, Julian lifted his head, looked at his cousin over her shoulder.

Rafi turned her head to meet Nico's gaze. His eyes studied her face even as he slid a hand deep into her hair and his lips found hers while Julian's mouth caressed her shoulder. She'd been barely aware of him drawing the shoulder of her dress aside so he could. Nico's arm tightened around her waist as they sank into the kiss.

Where Julian was bold and claimed her mouth possessively as his, Nico was more restrained. His tongue teased hers, toyed with it.

Even as he did, Rafi felt the scrape of Julian's teeth over the sensitive skin at the curve of her neck and shoulder, exposed now by the angle of her head as she kissed Nico.

It seemed as if her entire body turned molten, heated, at their touch. Julian's hand at her waist moved up, just a little. His thumb brushed the underside of her breast.

Rafi jolted as a shot of pure lust burst through her.

When Rafi made no move to stop him – in fact, her arm tightened around him even as she lifted a hand to cup Nico's cheek – Julian, emboldened, risked brushing his thumb over the crest of her breast, to feel her nipple taut beneath the silk.

His body went hotter and tighter in an instant and he groaned as, almost involuntarily, he closed his hand around that firm, ripe globe.

She quivered.

Nothing needed to be said.

Seduction was an old game between them, he and Nico.

The soft purr of the zipper of her dress going down and the cool, refreshing air against her heated skin was all Rafi felt. A hand, Nico's, slipped inside, slid around her stomach and up to curl around one breast as Julian caressed the other. All her awareness was suddenly centered around her nipples as they grew almost painfully tight while the two men played with them.

She moaned, softly.

A hand, Julian's she thought, expertly unhooked her bra. Nico's fingers slipped beneath the loosened lace to drift over her nipple to tease. She shivered as anticipatory pleasure raced through her.

His lips trailing across her shoulder, Julian gently guided the smooth silk over it. Inhaling the soft scent of her and her increasing excitement, he tasted her skin, his hunger for her growing by leaps and bounds. Circling an arm around her, he drew the silk from her other shoulder with his free hand.

Rafi's breasts were now free.

Without speaking, understanding what he needed, what they wanted, Rafi let her dress fall away with a sound not unlike the sigh escaping her.

Julian looked down at her in amazement even as Nico lifted his lips from Rafi's.

His eyes met his cousin's.

"Beautiful," he whispered, as he stroked a hand from her throat down over the curve of her breasts to send the bra the way of her dress.

She was bared to them now, save only for her thin lacy panties.

He tightened to see those pale globes with their rosy, taut tips revealed to them. Nico cupped the fullness of one breast in his hand and offered it to Julian.

Rafi watched as Julian lowered his head to take the offering Nico had made of her to him.

The sensation of Nico's hand around her breast, of Julian's warm mouth closing over her tight, aching nipple was almost unbearable. Her pussy dampened as Julian drew the tip of her breast into his mouth, sucked to take in more of it. Her hips bucked in response.

Nico watched as Rafi's nipple disappeared into Julian's mouth, the sight incredibly arousing. To feel Rafi tremble in his arms was even more so.

He loved this part of it, the dance of seduction and arousal, as much as Julian did.

With his eyes locked on his cousin's mouth on Rafi's breast, Nico caressed her taut belly, explored the indentation of her navel. He combed his fingers beneath the lace of her panties and through the tight curls between her thighs. He felt the crispness of those curls and the dampness between them.

He groaned as heat rushed through him so intensely his vision hazed.

Another hand joined his, Julian's, as Nico searched for the small bud nestled between Rafi's thighs to toy with it and found it.

She moaned, leaning back against him, the pressure of her body against his rigid cock maddening.

If only he wasn't so hungry.

Rafi drowned in a haze of erotic sensation, caught between the two men.

Then Nico touched her clit and a rush of pleasure shot through her, blanking her mind.

All she wanted was more, and more.

She got it.

As Nico teased her clit, she felt Julian's fingers stroke between the delicate folds of her labial lips teasingly. If she thought she'd been hot before, it seemed as if she'd turned incandescent. Desire pooled deep in her belly. Her hips pumped with need.

A single finger pierced her.

Pleasure so intense it was nearly painful speared through her and her body arched.

Julian was enraptured. Rafi's taste and scent filled him as he sucked on her breast, stroked a finger inside her. She was so sweet, so sensitive to each motion of his finger, so tight around it. He loved her openness. She gave of herself so completely.

If only he wasn't so hungry. He wanted to make love to her with Nico until she was limp and trembling with pleasure, until she couldn't move and they could feed at their leisure. And hers.

The rich scent of her arousal filled him. In wonder, Julian breathed it in.

Lifting his head, he looked at her. It was there in her eyes. Need. A need as great as their own.

His heart wrenched. It was a gift.

Rafi was nearly mindless, rapt in pleasure.

Another burst of heat shot through her, straight to her core. Her knees nearly buckled.

Insane as it was, she wanted it. She wanted them. Nearly desperately.

"We won't hurt you, Rafi. I swear it," Julian said, his dark-eyed gaze locked on hers. "We can make it very pleasant for you, I promise. It won't hurt for any longer than necessary."

Her eyes softened as she looked at him. She reached a hand out to Nico, understanding what it was they needed.

Nico looked at her in astonishment, knowing what it was she offered.

Herself.

"Just don't stop," she whispered, shakily.

"Dear God, no," Julian said, slipping his finger from inside her.

She moaned in protest until he slid two fingers inside her to stroke and she groaned.

Julian looked at Nico, who nodded.

If Rafi had thought she was lost before, the next moments proved her wrong, as Nico's fingers danced and toyed with her clit until her thighs quivered with each touch and Julian's long, agile fingers stroked inside her. Sensation poured through her. Nothing else mattered. Her heartbeat thundered in her ears.

Julian's mouth moved over her throat, his lips against her wildly beating pulse.

He could feel it throb beneath them. Desire throbbed deeper still because he knew she was willing.

Hunger moved within him, beat at him. But he was no animal to go ravening. He was the leader of the vampires here, the oldest and strongest of them. He had more control than that. It had been longer still since Nico had fed than he. Julian knew Nico had resorted to the less satisfying blood of animals rather than seek companionship and risk rejection, or worse, put Julian at risk. As hard as it had been on Julian, no matter the effort he took to make it pleasant for those he fed from, it was that much harder for Nico. He knew the craving had to be nearly painful, and yet like him Nico wanted to be sure, wanted Rafi to be sure, as Julian himself did.

Hunger raged, yet neither of them would take until they were certain.

Rafi looked at them, sensing their hesitation even as pleasure coursed through her in erotic waves.

What would it be like to feel Julian's warm mouth close over her throat, or Nico's? To feel their teeth penetrate? Another, different, kind of heat raced through her.

Deliberately, she turned her head, offered herself to them.

At her gesture, Julian bowed his head. Need was a pounding in his blood he couldn't deny, and he was grateful it wasn't necessary.

He lifted his gaze to Nico's. His cousin's eyes widened and Nico took a breath before he, too, nodded.

To Rafi's surprise, Julian lowered his mouth to her lips first, his kiss soft and sweet.

Even as he did so, Nico's fingers toyed with her nipple even as the fingers of his other hand played with her clit. But his cheek brushed her hair.

Long, skillful fingers moved inside her, to stroke.

Julian's lips brushed her eyelids, her cheek. His teeth nibbled at her earlobe even as his fingers worked inside her.

Pleasure enveloped her, blinded Rafi to anything but their touch.

Julian's mouth, not merely warm but hot now, closed over her throat as it had in her fantasies. His lips were on her skin, his teeth were poised, ready to strike, but giving her a moment to change her mind if that was what she chose.

It had always been her choice, each and every step of the way.

Julian's breath caressed her throat, as did his fangs, and sent goose bumps racing over her.

She felt his tongue lap lightly over her skin, to taste, yearning. It made her shiver. Heat speared through her like lightning, from her throat to her core. Her pussy clenched tightly around his fingers even as her nipples grew harder, if that were possible.

Was she really going to do it? If she didn't she was going to come any minute.

She could feel Julian's teeth. The sharp canines caressed her carotid artery as Nico's did her jugular. Sensation sent another swift jolt of exhilaration through her.

Rafi's body throbbed, became one aching pulse point as they stroked and teased her. Pleasure ran through her in waves, building as they guided her to a settee, eased her down onto it. Suddenly, nothing else mattered other than the sweet bliss that gathered inside her. She quivered, her body tightening as ecstasy welled within her.

She looked at them, at the need in their eyes, and reached up to stroke Nico's face, turned her wrist to offer it to him.

In wonder, he took it, brushed his lips over the sensitive skin. The fingers of his free hand danced on her clit. Her body bowed as pleasure filled her.

At the same moment their teeth pierced her skin with a gentle pop at throat and wrist, an ephemeral flash of pain. For a moment there was only the sensation of their warm mouths against her skin. A shiver went through her. It felt shockingly good.

Then they suckled.

Her body bucked with intense pleasure.

Both drew deeply, one quick mouthful.

Ecstasy blinded her, speared into her depths and she cried out softly in wonder, in glorious bliss. Julian hadn't lied about that. They could indeed make it pleasurable. Now she understood those girls in the bars.

She looked at Nico, his eyes closed as he relished the taste of her. Another shot of pleasure raced straight to her core at the sight.

Julian's mouth was locked on her throat, savoring her.

That first mouthful was a wonder to Julian, a joy. She tasted marvelously rich, sweet and clean. Her pleasure surged through her and into him. He shuddered as the taste of her swept through him.

So hungry, he was so very hungry and she was so gloriously sweet, so rich, so delicious. He relished her, basked in the taste of her. If she was this good now, what would she be like when her blood had been truly heated? *Dear god.* He shuddered in anticipatory delight.

If she stayed.

Lifting his mouth from her, his gaze went to Nico, watching as his cousin's eyelids slid closed with his own pleasure.

As he watched, Nico's eyes fluttered with a matching satisfaction and Julian knew his cousin felt the same incredible pleasure race through his body even as it poured through his own.

Finally, they could feed without fear.

So good.

He only wished the hunger, the need, wasn't so great. They would have taken their time, pleasured Rafi more deeply first and part of him couldn't wait to do so, to take her with his body as he did with his teeth. Even now as he slid his arm around her slender waist to draw her closer he couldn't resist letting the back of his hand brush the underside of her breast. A part of him was all too aware of how her body felt beneath his hand, against him. Her blood heated at his touch as he pleasured her.

He settled his mouth over her again, let his fangs penetrate. Her hot blood coursed into his mouth.

The taste of her grew richer, more vibrant and Julian closed his eyes in wonder. Her taste revealed the truth, revealed her growing delight at the feel of them both feeding from her.

Control vanished as she quivered in his arms.

An intense rush of pleasure, of heat, raced through Julian to Rafi, shot straight to her core, and Rafi's body bucked in reaction as she heard Julian groan in ecstasy, felt the vibration of that sound against her throat.

Finally, he fed in earnest, pulling mouthfuls from her, each one sending a shot of electricity straight through her to her core, to her pussy. In that moment she wouldn't have cared if they did suck her dry, she was in heaven.

Through pleasure-hazed eyes Rafi looked at Nico, his expression nearly despairing with need and then his mouth closed more tightly over her wrist. He drank, deeply. Pleasure spiked through her. He started to feed as well, drawing a great hungry draught of her into his mouth. His eyes closed, the lids fluttered. She watched as he, too, savored the taste of her. It sent a thrill through her.

He started to drink nearly frantically, his throat working.

Julian's arms encircled her gently but as strong as steel, his mouth working on her throat. Sucking. Sucking hard.

This was real. And it was wonderful. She trembled as pleasure poured through her.

She surrendered to it. To them.

Helpless between them, there was nothing she could do except let them feed…deliriously. Lost in the pleasure of it, she felt Julian's hand on her chest, over her heart, pressing there to feel her heart beat beneath it as she quivered in delight.

Even as it seemed they drank her life away and a touch of fear speared through her, a deeper, darker pleasure slid alongside it. They could indeed make it pleasurable. Ecstasy shot to her core, flooded it.

Darkness closed around her vision. With a blissful sigh, she let it take her.

Julian and Nico drank until Rafi went limp – until they were, if not sated, at least not so very hungry. Julian cradled her against him. Nico licked the wound in her wrist closed as he looked at Julian.

Worried, Nico said, "Did we take too much?"

When she'd reached out for him, offered herself to him, those piercing blue eyes softening, something inside him had...shifted.

He'd watched her face as he'd bit down, as her hot blood gushed into his mouth. Looking into her blue eyes, he could see she'd known, been aware of him, had felt his teeth pierce her, his mouth on her, deliriously sucking in great drafts of her blood. She'd enjoyed it, her pretty lips parting, her eyelids drifting closed over those brilliant eyes.

If Julian was right, if she could take them both, they could pleasure her in many ways. They would give her whatever she wanted.

Nico wanted her now in another way. With his hunger eased, other needs arose. Now though, was not the time.

Taking a breath, lifting Rafi into his arms, Julian shook his head.

"I don't think so. Not now. The first few days will be the hardest. We must drain her fairly deeply. Not so much that her veins collapse but enough that her body compensates. In a few weeks I believe she'll feed us both with ease. We simply have to condition her to it."

It might be pleasant. He hoped it would be and would try to make it so. He hoped she wouldn't change her mind.

Gently, he brushed a kiss over her pale forehead.

"I like her, Julian," Nico said.

He remembered her bright laughter as she'd come in the door, her compassion at his need.

There had been some - many - over the centuries who hadn't been as kind as she. He would bear the scars of that forever.

If he'd suffered, how much more had Julian, who bore greater and deeper scars than his?

Then there was Rafi.

In only a moment he'd fallen in love with those clear blue eyes.

Julian looked at the woman in his arms, her lovely eyes closed. He'd fallen in love with her the moment she'd laughed.

They had indeed chosen well. He thought they would all suit each other very well. Very well indeed.

"As do I, Nico," Julian answered softly.

Chapter Five

THERE WERE FAR WORSE ways to wake up than with two hard sexy male bodies pressed against her to keep her warm, Rafi thought. Many, many worse ways, especially since both seemed to be cuddlers, unusual in men these days. For once she hadn't awakened alone. Julian had an arm around her, his hand cupped around her breast and a leg curled around one of hers as she snuggled back against him. Her head was pillowed on Nico's arm with Nico's hand on her hip, his cheek against her hair.

She was also very naked, one of her favorite ways to be.

So were they.

That had its pleasures too. She sighed, delighted to enjoy the view. She'd suspected they were very well-built, nicely muscled men beneath their clothes, their muscles toned, their bodies fit.

She'd been more than right.

From what she could see of the exposed skin beneath tangled sheets, bodies and limbs, they were beautiful. Of the two Julian was the leaner, the curve of the muscles of his chest strong, while Nico was more solid. Both had excellent pecs, taut abs and long, muscular legs.

Julian's breath was warm against her throat.

Speaking of which...

Rafi did a quick mental assessment. She'd expected to feel a little weak, a little headachy, but there was nothing. She felt fine. She was alive. She'd taken the leap and survived.

Again.

She readily admitted to being an adrenaline junky, but not reckless about it.

A thrill went through her as she remembered the two of them feeding on her the night before. In an instant her pussy was damp and aching. It had been so incredibly erotic to feel their mouths on her. To her astonishment, she already wanted them to feed on her again, to experience that incredible rush once more.

She felt Julian stir, his arm tighten around her.

Julian woke slowly, unusual for him of late. His mouth brushed Rafi's throat. Beneath his lips her pulse beat regularly and steadily, and he breathed a sigh of relief. He placed a gentle kiss there as he closed his hand more tightly around the curve of her full breast. She felt wonderful. Almost unconsciously, only half awake, he stroked and squeezed, the lush weight of her breast sweet in his palm.

His cock hardened but he could have played with her breast for hours, massaging and caressing it as her nipple stiffened beneath his hand, between his fingers.

Still in all honor, he had to wake her first. He was and would always remain an honorable man. The centuries might pass and honor go in and out of style but he wouldn't change. He needed her consent.

Then he felt her shift to accommodate him and realized she was already awake.

"How do you feel?" he asked softly. "Are you all right?"

Not that he wasn't reasonably certain of it, most made the transition without difficulty, her body adjusting to the changes passed to her by their feeding while they slept.

She smiled a little and said reassuringly, "I'm fine."

"You can still leave," he said, keeping his voice carefully even, "if you choose."

He didn't want to influence her.

Nico had scruples as well, just not that one. He stroked her hip idly. "But we would very much like you to stay."

So Nico was awake, too.

Rafi looked up into his golden-brown eyes, saw the intense look in them. Turning her head, she met Julian's darker gaze again. His expression, to her surprise, was softer.

With Julian playing with her nipple and Nico stroking her hip it was difficult for her to concentrate. Unsurprisingly, she discovered she also had two heavy, very hard male erections pressed against her.

Two.

Heat shot through her at the thought.

She looked from Julian's lean, strong, handsome face to Nico's fuller, younger one.

"It would be much easier to say no if you'd stop doing what you're doing," she said. "But I don't want to go and I don't want you to stop."

Julian smiled and her heart stuttered a little at the sight of it. Rafi let out a breath. He had a wonderful smile did Julian. Beautiful.

So did Nico, although his was a little more impish, more playful now.

"You like this?" Julian asked.

His hand closed over her breast, trapped her nipple between finger and thumb. It felt delicious when he pinched it lightly, sending a shot of heat like lightning straight to her core.

Rafi arched a brow at him as her nipple tightened at his touch.

"What do you think?"

Julian's smile became a grin as he rolled her hardening nipple between his fingers, his leg curling around hers as he let her head settle into the curve of his shoulder.

She allowed the back of her hand to fall against the curves of the muscles of his chest, felt the crisp hair there brush against her fingers.

Nico wrapped one his legs around her free one, claiming her as well.

Cupping her breast, this time Julian held it for Nico.

Rafi's throat tightened. Something about that gesture...shattered her. It couldn't have said more clearly that they wanted to share her. All the breath went out of her as a rush of excitement speared through her.

Nico lowered his head to take Julian's offering and he sipped to draw her now tightly furled nipple into his mouth as Julian brushed his lips over hers. He kissed her sweetly and deeply as Nico nibbled and suckled on the tender tip of her breast. The combination of sensations, gentle and stirring, was marvelous.

She stroked Nico's hair, running her fingers through it.

Nico sighed, sliding up her body to take his turn kissing her. Her tender gesture sent a wave of gratitude and amazement through him. So simple, and yet it was everything for which he'd waited, everything he wanted. This was what they'd missed, simple affection as well as the greater.

As Julian propped his head on his hand, Nico tasted her lips gently with a light brush of his tongue. With only that, they parted for him. He thanked the gods for her responsiveness. Heat moved through him as he took her mouth to taste her deeply and was delighted when her tongue swept around his in a gentle caress. He sighed again in pure pleasure as he felt her lips curve in a smile at the taste of him.

To have Nico's mouth on hers while Julian touched her was an entirely new experience for Rafi. One she welcomed.

Nico tasted sweet and clean. Where Julian's tongue had speared into her mouth to claim it as his own, Nico requested. His hand drifted over her so lightly she barely felt his soft caress as anything more than a whisper of electric heat over her skin.

Julian molded her other breast in his hand, played with and teased it.

Shots of heat raced through her with each pinch and tug on her nipple.

Julian's blood went hot, his cock going hard at her smile of pleasure even as she shifted her body more tightly against his.

It was almost a shock to realize he could have her, that they both could.

She was hardly the first woman he'd touched or pleasured, but the idea they could both take her, they could share her, sent a shot of heat through him. In the past, they'd had to pay for the pleasure, and there was a coldness, a calculation, to the act that had a chilling effect on him.

Not here. Rafi trembled at their touch, soft cries of pleasure escaping her.

Tentatively, Nico explored her with hands and fingers, heat moving through him with each touch, each quiver of her body. The ache in his cock grew as she murmured her delight against his mouth.

Watching Julian play with Rafi's nipple and then offer him her breast had been incredible.

He brushed his palm over the crest of one breast, traced the shape of it with the tips of his fingers as she shivered before sliding his hand down over her stomach to brush over the delicate curls between her thighs. The scent of her growing excitement filled the air like a heady incense, increasing his own desire.

Julian's mouth brushed Rafi's shoulder, watching as Nico kissed her, touched her. An expression close to wonder lit his cousin's face as Nico began, hesitantly, to explore. Watching his cousin's fingers dance over Rafi's curves, over her smooth belly, only made Julian himself harder as he stroked her breast.

He pressed his throbbing shaft against her hip, watching Rafi's expression as intently as he did Nico's. There was a kind of wonder on her face to match their own.

Rafi shivered as Nico's fingers combed lightly through the curls of her mound, so close to her clit, the light touch setting her blood afire and awakening the ache deep in her pussy. Her thighs grew damp.

Nico lifted his lips from hers to admire her body and observe as Julian toyed with her nipple.

Watching them as they touched her sent even more heat pouring through Rafi.

She felt Nico's cock twitch against one hip while Julian's pressed hard against the other.

She could see the growing passion in Julian's eyes, in the intensity of his gaze, everything focused on the way their bodies touched. His hand squeezed her breast more and more tightly. Nico played with the curls between her thighs, coming close, so close, to the little nub there, and to her core. That tantalizing touch was driving her crazy. His expression was fascinated as her hips pumped in response to her need.

Her clit throbbed with his fingers so close, his touch so delicate.

Then Julian's mouth closed over her other breast, sucked her nipple into his mouth. The sudden pleasure of it was almost shocking in its intensity, drawing a moan from her as her pussy clenched in response. His leg tightened around one of hers to draw her closer to him, his erection pressed hard against her hip. His hips thrust to grind it against her.

That was the difference between the two men. Julian was more demanding, more aggressive, like his kisses. Nico was gentler, the more tentative of the two, for all his bold stride and intensity.

Watching them as they teased and tormented her was incredible, more erotic than she could have imagined. Feeling their touch, their lips, tongues, and fingers on her, was maddening.

Julian loved her breasts. He'd always been a breast man. As he'd undressed her the night before, he'd admired them. They were full, firm, and nicely rounded, the areola large but not too large, really lovely. The taste of them, the feel of her nipples as they stiffened against his tongue was delicious. He couldn't resist suckling them, nibbling on them a little to make her writhe. And she did.

That was promising. There was only one question left now to answer.

First, though, there was time to explore. To savor and enjoy. He wouldn't waste it. There was no need to rush. Julian wanted to take his time and explore every inch of her with every inch of him.

He breathed in the scent of her arousal, his cock as hard as rock.

Catching that stiff nipple between his teeth, he nipped it, then scraped them over it, drawing it upward. He felt her hand in his hair, it dropped to his shoulder to clutch at him when he nibbled. He caught that hand, pinned it to the bed above her head.

Even as he did, he watched Nico play with her, touch her, and his cock stiffened even more to see Nico's hands tease her, make her tremble.

Rafi felt as if she would lose her mind with pleasure.

Both men stroked her, caressed her breasts and played with her nipples, teased them, rolled and pinched them until those sensitive nubs were aching and as hard as pebbles, it seemed. Julian used just his fingertips, let them float over her skin to make her shiver while Nico's palm drifted warmly just above her skin, barely grazing it. Now and then one or the other of them slid their hands over her stomach, stroked her thighs, dipped their fingers between them to tease and tantalize. Her body quivered and arched to each touch.

She pulsed with need, wanting to be filled, to be taken.

They took turns kissing her, sucking on her, all of her. Their warm mouths moved over her throat, brushed lightly over her ears to nibble at the lobes, before one or the other of them returned to her mouth to taste, to devour, then to her breasts, down her belly. They sought out her erogenous zones, licking, nibbling and sucking until she was gasping, wet and aching. Their cocks were heavy against her thighs.

Just the thought of one of those thick shafts penetrating her made her want to moan. The idea that both of them would take her made her pussy clench and ache, her thighs go damper.

Every inch of her skin seemed to be on fire. Her breasts felt heavy, swollen, her nipples as hard as diamonds. In all her life she'd never ached so much, longed so much to be filled, to have a cock buried deep inside her.

With a knowing glance and a grin at Julian, Nico bent to kiss her belly as Julian curled his leg tighter around Rafi's to shift her a little.

She saw Julian grin back.

Delirious with pleasure, she still managed to give them a wary, amused look.

Nico shifted down the length of her body as Julian drew her legs even further apart and she realized what he was doing, what they were doing.

She found she was helpless, spread for Nico like a banquet with Julian's leg curled around hers to keep her legs open while Nico gently pressed her thighs even farther apart. He slid his hands beneath her to cup her ass, tilted her hips to open her to him.

Pure need speared deep into her belly as Nico carefully parted the curls between her thighs with his thumbs, parted the delicate folds of her pussy and then lowered his head to breathe in the scent of her arousal. Then his tongue touched her, tasted her with just the lightest flick of his tongue against her sensitized clit.

A sharp jolt of pleasure speared through her at that delicate touch. She moaned and very nearly cried out as it shot through her.

The two men looked at each other and smiled.

Nico sighed as he lay between Rafi's shapely thighs. The rich, musky scent of her pleasure filled him. Lovely. He smiled when she twitched in response to the barest touch.

Delicately, he swept his tongue slowly and deeply between the delicate folds, driving a low moan of pleasure from her.

Nico truly loved eating pussy but to his delight he found he loved eating Rafi's even more. He loved giving that pleasure to a woman, but to Rafi? That was different. She was so incredibly sensitive. Each slide of his tongue over her lower lips made her tighten, her back bow, her breath catch. Her body quivered with each flick of his tongue on her clit. The muscles in her belly and thighs twitched at each touch.

Julian loved her responsiveness. He curled an arm around her to hold her securely in place as he brushed gentle kisses over her face. He played with her swollen breasts, her tightly furled nipples, as Nico settled in to savor her, knowing how much his cousin enjoyed this particular act. He had his own pleasures and intended to take them.

While Nico licked and savored, Rafi felt Julian's mouth close over first one nipple, then the other, to nip and suck.

Delicious heat poured through her as Nico slid his clever tongue up to swirl around her clit, to tease it with quick, light flicks. She wailed softly as torrents of pleasure ran through her with each delicate touch. His mouth closed on her pussy and pleasure poured though her as his warm tongue laved her deeply. The sensation was incredible. He fucked her with his tongue, something she'd never experienced, sucking on her, suckling on her, devouring her.

She quivered as he and Julian tormented her in ways she'd only ever dreamed of but wished could be real.

Nico savored her, the rich cream of her, the musky scent of her arousal exciting, enticing him. Sliding his tongue deep inside her as she moaned, he suckled on her to draw it out. With each motion of his tongue, he watched vibrant color sweep beneath her skin. No woman had ever responded to him as freely as she did. It was incredible.

She was lost in what they did to her, her eyes unfocused.

What would it be like to tie her down so she couldn't wiggle and writhe as she did now? If she were spread, helpless to prevent him, with every muscle taut, her hands clutching the ropes or scarves as he devoured her? Just the thought made him shiver in anticipation.

He drove her up to the heights of pleasure, delighted as he felt the muscles of her belly tighten, her thighs quiver with each stroke of his tongue across her clit. Moans and soft cries escaped her as her body strained against Julian's implacable grip while Julian's teeth and fingers tugged on her tightly furled nipples.

Settling his mouth over her clit, Nico swiftly pushed two fingers inside her, found and then stroked her g-spot. He took a breath and drew her clit into his mouth again, suckling.

Rafi's eyelids fluttered, her body shuddered helplessly beneath his erotic assault.

Nico wanted to hear her scream with pleasure, her body open for him in offering.

He would take her soon knowing Julian would watch as he did it. The idea was intensely exciting.

Deliberately, he swirled his tongue around her sensitive clit where his lips held it trapped.

A long low wail escaped her, building as he sucked on her with increasing intensity.

Rafi surrendered as her orgasm built, her legs opened for him, quivering helplessly.

"This can be just for your pleasure," Julian said against her ear.

Rafi trembled, nearly speechless at the thought of him feeding from her at the same time Nico ate her pussy. She curled her hand around his head to draw his mouth down against her throat.

"Please," she whispered, need rushing through her.

She wanted that delicious ecstasy, as Julian fed on her with hard pulls at her throat. And with Nico eating her pussy? She was in heaven as each stroke of Nico's tongue sent shots of heat rippling through her.

Pressing a kiss against her hammering pulse, Julian breathed, "Thank you."

No,...thank you, she thought as his mouth closed over her throat.

He didn't stop playing with her nipples, for which she was grateful. His long fingers tugged and pinched them as he held her gently immobile.

She quivered helplessly, her body instinctively trying to escape the carnal torture that drew cry after cry from her.

Each flick and sweep of Nico's tongue over her clit and his fingers in her core, stroking her g-spot, had her muscles jumping in response, each a sharp burst of pleasure, building on the last as her orgasm grew, swelled within her.

Rafi nearly wept from the pleasure that swept through her in waves.

Sensation from Julian's hands teasing her breasts and Nico's mouth on her clit, his fingers inside her, streamed through her, pooled, built.

Her mind went blank, her entire body awash as ecstasy gathered within her like a tightly wound spring. She cried out as Nico's tongue flicked her clit. Then Julian bit into her throat, and the sensation of his mouth on her, his teeth penetrating her, added another layer of pleasure. Ecstasy burst free, roared through her. She went rigid, shuddering, crying out in delirious bliss.

It seemed to Rafi that her orgasm would never stop, pleasure rolled through her in huge, deep waves as she quivered wildly with each swallow, each soft tug on her throat from Julian as Nico sucked at her pussy.

Nico watched her, watched Julian.

The look on Julian's face as he fed was all the answer Nico needed. But he was hard, incredibly hard, and the taste and sound of Rafi's pleasure was driving him crazy. He loved that she would let them hear it but it was too much. Control vanished.

Surging up, Nico drove his cock deep into the hot, tight wetness where his tongue had been, his fingers had been, only moments before. Her slick internal muscles clenched around his throbbing member as he thrust it deeply into her. She felt incredible.

He buried his shaft inside her all the way to the hilt, balls-deep.

It...she, was wonderful. So tight, so hot and so very wet.

Nico smiled as she tightened around him. Her muscles still quivered from her orgasm, stroking him. All he wanted to do was fuck her, pound into her and he did, her cries of pleasure like spurs to his thrusts, driving him onward.

His own orgasm erupted through him as he emptied into her.

Marvelous. She was marvelous. Sweet and intoxicating.

Julian had to force himself to stop, to take enough for the pleasure of the taste of her and the rush her ecstasy gave him as well as her. Nico had yet to feed as well.

Licking his lips to savor the taste for just a moment longer, Julian held Rafi gently as she quivered with pleasure, watched Nico as he took her. Another cry of pleasure burst out of her at the sensation of Nico's cock inside her. Nico's eyes closed as his body arched and he thrust inside her, his cock buried deep, his hips pistoned against her.

Soon, Julian would also take her, he longed to feel her sweet pussy close around him, too.

Julian looked at Rafi, her lovely eyes closed, her expression ecstatic. She smiled as Nico drove his cock into her. That smile astonished him.

Opening her eyes, Rafi saw Julian looking at her tenderly. Nico was poised above her like a beautiful marble statue, his cock buried deep within her. His gorgeous body went taut as he froze, his hips locked to hers as he pumped his hot cum inside her. Every lean muscle of that beautiful body was tight - the muscles of his strong shoulders were bunched, his head was thrown back. As incredible as he felt inside her, he looked even more beautiful above her as he emptied himself and his heat filled her.

A breath shuddered out of her.

Julian dropped a light kiss on her lips and then Nico did too, as his orgasm released him, his hips thrusting against hers.

She reached up to touch their faces, her fingers trembling.

"That was incredible," she said.

Nodding, Julian said, "Definitely. You are marvelous, Raffia, on many, many levels. But we're not done. It's my turn."

Julian shifted and Nico moved to take his place.

"I can't," she said, laughing weakly. "It's not possible. I'm too limp to move."

She'd never had two orgasms in a row, much less three.

Julian looked at her as some men would eye a good steak or fine caviar. A shot of lust burst through her.

Again? So soon? Be careful what you wish for, was all she could think, laughing to herself.

With a smile, Julian moved down to slide his hands between and beneath her thighs to cup her bottom and lift her, angling her for his own pleasure.

As always Nico had done a good job, her clit was still swollen. It would be extremely sensitive.

Watching had been maddening. His cock was like iron - thick, throbbing.

His breath feathered lightly over delicate tissues. Julian felt her quiver and smiled.

"We will know very soon," he promised.

He was hungry for her. The scent of her satisfaction was ripe in the air. Julian breathed her in, closing his eyes in pleasure as Nico held her, pressed a gentle kiss by the corner of her eye. Nico's long fingers played over her breasts, and her nipples tightened.

She watched him as he lowered his mouth to her clit, gave it a gentle brush of his tongue as he slipped two fingers inside her, deep, to stroke gently and then with increasing pressure. His eyes never left hers.

He wanted her to see, to watch him eat her clit as Nico played with her nipples, Nico's mouth soft against her throat, his tongue tasting her skin.

She pressed a hand over his, over the one on her hip, the one holding her still, and brushed her other hand across Nico's muscled chest as she turned her head for Nico to present her throat to him.

Offering herself to Nico as she had to Julian. Julian went iron-hard in an instant.

He watched her eyelids flutter, felt the muscles inside her jump with each flick of his tongue. He wanted her now, intensely. Wanted her heated pleasure to close around his throbbing, aching cock. In all his long life he couldn't remember ever being this hard. The need to possess her was nearly overwhelming.

First, he wanted to give her and Nico this.

He licked her, lapped at her clit, swirled his tongue over it, driving her up, his fingers inside her stroking as Nico's fingers played, tightening on her nipples. His tongue touched her already sensitized clit and she arched. He looked at Nico and nodded. He held her in place as Nico's teeth pierced her and ecstasy shot through her again.

She was incredible, better than either of them had thought possible. He watched Nico as Rafi's blood burst into his mouth and he drank her essence. Nico trembled as the glorious taste of her exploded in his mouth. So did Rafi.

The sight of her beautiful body quivering with pleasure, the pleasure they gave her, was more than Julian could bear. He had to have her, now.

Surging up, Julian did as Nico had and drove his cock deep inside her in one hard thrust, her wet heat clenching around him.

Rafi cried out as Julian took her fast and hard. He filled her, stretched her more than Nico had, his cock thicker than Nico's as it rammed up inside her. She moaned with pure bliss as he stretched her, smiled in ecstasy as he hammered into her while Nico fed.

It was intense, shattering, to have both of them take their pleasure of her this way.

Julian thrust into her deeply.

This. This was what she'd been looking for all these years.

It was as if she'd died and gone to heaven.

A delicious lassitude swept through her as she trembled and shook, as Julian swelled inside her, stretching her further. She cried out as another orgasm shot through her.

Her eyes opened at the sound of Julian's groan, to find him arched above her as Nico had been, his shaft buried inside her, his lean, muscular body sharply defined as he went taut. He was glorious, primal in his ecstasy. It was like being taken by some ancient Sumerian god.

Julian drove up hard inside her, his strong body shuddering as he erupted, filled her with his hot cum, a long low groan escaping him.

Nico moaned as he drank from her, filled his mouth with her. The second burst of her pleasure was even better than the first. He lifted his lips from her throat, licked it before he brushed a kiss over her temple.

She shivered a little.

"Rafi, love?" Julian said, eyeing her.

Rafi smiled at him.

In all her life she'd never felt so completely sated, so totally and wonderfully used. Her heart still pounded but she supposed that was to be expected.

"I think she liked it," Nico said, smiling in return.

Rafi looked at him, tried to speak and had to clear her throat before trying again.

"You could say that," she said, her voice a whisper.

"So did we. Very much."

To her astonishment, Julian carried her into the bathroom as Nico went ahead to start the water running in the huge marble tub. She was too drained to stand, much less wash herself. Instead, they washed her. The warm water was heavenly, as were their soapy, slick hands on her body.

It felt wonderful.

"Don't get too used to this," Julian teased, kissing her on the nose. "We won't need to do this once you become conditioned to us."

She grinned. "But you don't mind if I enjoy it now?"

"Oh no," he said, his hands slipping over her skin. "No, not at all."

Chapter Six

THE HOUSE WAS SIMPLY immense. It was like playing hide and go seek, or a treasure hunt in some ancient king's castle. With Julian, that wouldn't have been much of a surprise, Rafi thought with a smile. She wandered the halls, exploring, shaking her head in sheer astonishment. Other than the bedroom they shared that morning and one other, clearly Nico's by the number of computer books, none of the other bedrooms seemed to have been occupied in some time.

She'd slept for hours, waking only when a very shy maid brought in a tray of food. It was a good thing she was off-duty for the night. She just never expected it to go quite as well as it had. Her body went warm at the memories of the previous night and morning.

The scent of coffee on the tray the maid brought beckoned to her. Beside the plate was a newspaper. Servants. All the comforts of home. Rafi shook her head. Not her home.

Ducking her head and smiling, the maid said, "Mr. Julian, he said to tell you to take your time and ask anyone if you wish to find him. Your things are here. There are fresh towels in the bathroom and clothing has been set out for you."

The woman gestured to an armoire and left.

So, Rafi took her time, lifting the lid from the plate, amazed to find her stomach cramping as she looked at the food. She blinked. Scrambled eggs, ham, three kinds of toast and jams, along with a fruit and yogurt parfait. It was too much, far more than the usual bagel and coffee she usually had. The smell was heavenly.

She ate while she read the newspapers, found her cell phone to check her e-mail and looked around the room.

It was huge and plush. Damask draperies framed the windows, thick cords held them back. She'd never seen a bed as big as the one on which she sat. It had to have been custom made it was so large, yet it hadn't seemed that big with the three of them in it. The thick duvet that covered her lap was a contrasting material to the drapes.

She laughed to herself. She felt oddly like a princess.

To her shock she realized that, distracted, she'd eaten every bite of the food.

Stepping into the bathroom again had been like walking into a sybarite's delight. The bath was the size of a small pond, easily large enough to fit several people, while the shower had been one of those multi-head, massage and sauna combinations. It felt like heaven to have the water pound over all her stretched and delightfully strained muscles.

Then she'd dressed and wandered as she scrunched her damp hair.

Continuing her exploration, she opened another door, this one on the lower floor, to find a long, dark, wood-paneled room with high clerestory windows. It looked like nothing else than an ancient dining hall. An antique refectory table stretched nearly the length of the room and could easily seat twenty people. Beside it was a long serving table. Beneath was another thick Persian rug over a wood floor. Real wood by the look and the wear of it.

The next room simply took her breath away.

Circular, it was surprisingly large and yet still managed to be cozy somehow.

Between the large windows with their views of the city below was coffered wood paneling that covered all the walls but one, and that one had a fireplace with a broad marble mantle stretched over it. A portrait, clearly of Julian, yet just as clearly centuries old by the armor and clothing he wore, hung above it.

The floor was covered by another Persian carpet, this one clearly old, worn and somehow comfortable. A desk of some dark wood with reddish undertones, maybe mahogany, filled one end. Two upholstered wing chairs with a small table in front and between them, sat before the fire. On the table was a tray with an etched glass decanter filled with some golden liquid, probably whiskey. Beside the decanter were four small glasses.

Brilliant sunlight filled the room.

This was where the butler - a butler, for heaven's sake - a very nice man by the name of Gordon, had told her she would find Julian.

In Julian's study.

Find him she did.

He stood by one of the windows, his dark head a little bowed, papers in his hand.

Once more her breath caught, but this time at the sight of him.

Sunlight gleamed brilliantly from his black hair, illuminating the strong features of his face and his firm mouth. He wore a silk shirt loose and unbuttoned over a pair of matching silk lounging pants, the open shirt revealing the curved muscles of his chest and his washboard abs.

Her mouth watered almost instantly just at the sight of him. She wanted to devour every inch of his body. She went hot and wet in an instant at the memory of his cock inside her, the way it had stretched her, filled her. It had been a long time since she'd been with anyone, and her craving for him, for Nico, was nearly insatiable. She didn't know how long this would last, but she intended to make the most of it.

"Just how rich are you?" she asked.

Whatever apprehensions she might have had about the situation fled at the warmth in his eyes when he saw her standing there.

Julian looked up and smiled, just at the sight of her, both amused at her question and heartened. Most women in the circles he traveled never mentioned money, it was considered unseemly, yet all of them found ways to determine it. He found Rafi's directness and honesty refreshing.

"Very," he answered. Instantly he set his papers aside and went to her. "In fact, I spend a great deal of my time advising other very rich men on how to invest their money. Which is enough to satisfy a number of institutions on the matter of how I came by my own."

It had become more and more necessary over the decades to find such explanations. That was the only up side to the current situation regarding paranormals. At least now such trivialities wouldn't be necessary. It would also just make men like him somewhat easier to find.

He shook off his presentiments. That was for tomorrow and would come soon enough. For now, he had far more pressing matters. Rafi.

It was clear she'd just showered, she smelled fresh and clean, and looked heavenly. Desire tugged deep.

"Raffia," he said, a moment before he slid his hands into her hair and took her mouth.

That kiss erased the last of Rafi's doubts.

He didn't just kiss her, he devoured her, that incredible mouth of his covered hers fiercely, possessed it, his tongue going deep as one hand curled in her hair while the other slid down her back to draw her body close and hard against him.

Rafi let out a long sigh and simply drowned in the taste of him, her tongue tangling with his, every inch of her body going hot as she slid her hand up into his silky hair to pull his mouth harder against hers. She could feel the strong muscles of his chest against her breasts, separated from her only by the silk dress someone - probably Julian - had laid out for her. Her nipples pebbled at the feel of those hard muscles against her.

Clearly reluctant to do so, he pulled a little away to cup his hand lightly around her cheek.

"How do you feel?" he asked, worry for her clear in his dark eyes.

With a little shrug, she said, reassuringly, "Not much different from when I've given blood."

She felt a little weak, a little achy, but much, much better standing in his arms. That connection was still there.

The relief in his eyes was a match to her own.

"The sunshine thing?" she asked, with a wave at the sunny room around her before returning her hand to his chest to stroke.

"Another myth," he said, smiling, keeping his arm around her waist, his muscles tightening to draw her closer as she caressed him. "After the rise of some religions that named us demons, as I said, it became easier to hunt at night. Over time even among ourselves some struggled with the change, believing the stories, and went into seclusion, giving credence to that myth."

His blue eyes heated as his gaze went to her hand where she ran it over his chest, spreading her fingers to try to span the broad muscle there. She couldn't, it just wasn't possible. Her hand wasn't big enough.

"I love your chest," she said, enjoying the pleasure of just touching him.

Amused, laughter lighting his eyes, he said, "As I love yours, Raffia," dropping his gaze to admire the curves of her breasts revealed by the deep V of her dress. Her nipples stood out clearly against the thin material, already hard. Between her thighs he knew she could feel clear evidence of his attraction - his long, thick cock was rigid against her mound.

He shifted his hips a little and she looked up at him with a grin, knowing he wanted her to feel it.

"So, have you been exploring?"

"This house is huge," she said.

"I can't take credit for the building itself, it was already here," Julian said, "I wanted privacy, and acreage, and a place to grow grapes. We can take a tour of the grounds later, if you'd like."

"I'd like that very much."

Nico walked in, his face brightening when he saw them, and he came over to kiss her too. Julian kept his arm around her so she was sandwiched between the two of them as Nico's mouth covered hers, his hand curling around her waist.

Even as Nico kissed her, Julian's mouth moved over her bare shoulder, his hand sliding the silk away to expose it, his lips following the fabric.

Nico's firm mouth moved on hers gently, his tongue danced lightly over hers and she opened to him. His tongue slipped deep between them as he slid his hand into her hair to cup her head and hold it while he gently savored her. His mouth was as talented on hers as it had been when he had eaten her pussy. She'd be hard pressed to say which of the two men was the better kisser.

Obligingly, Nico tightened his hold on her waist so she could arch back against him as Julian's free hand slid beneath her breast to cup it, his thumb brushing across the hardened nub beneath the silk. Nico shifted to settle his hardening erection between the cheeks of her ass, his hips undulating against her, driving hers against Julian's.

"This is ridiculous," she murmured. "I can't seem to get enough of you, either of you. It's as if I'm in heat."

Julian grinned. "In a way, you are, your body is answering your desire as you change."

Concerned, he looked at her.

"Do you mind?"

Rafi shook her head. "How could I? Besides I think it's as much that as like being a kid with new toys, I just want to keep playing with them."

Both Julian and Nico laughed.

"Play away," Nico said.

She sighed with pleasure, looking from one to the other, puzzled, questioning. It amazed her that there seemed to be no jealousy between them. She just couldn't find the words to ask.

With a shrug and a smile, Julian said, in answer to her unasked question, "We grew up together. Nico was the younger brother I never had. We shared almost everything. Over the centuries, fighting beside each other, watching out for each other, we've only grown closer. We didn't want to be forced to choose between one or the other. This is no different. This was what we were seeking."

His fingers traced the line of her jaw.

"Besides," Nico said, brushing his mouth over the curve of her throat and shoulder, "we both like you very much."

She shivered with pleasure at the feel of his soft mouth on her, reaching up to curl an arm backward over his neck. His free hand slid up her thigh beneath the dress. She felt his lips curve against her throat as he found nothing there to impede him. Julian hadn't laid out any underwear, so she'd worn none.

Heat flooded her pussy with his fingers so close.

"As I like you both very much," she said, sliding other hand over Julian's hip to close around the tight curve of his ass and pull him closer.

Julian groaned, his cock as hard as steel. "Gods, Rafi, do you know how much I want you?"

Leaning back, he showed her, the thin silk of his lounging pants tented over a very impressive erection.

Watching her expression as she reached for him - the wonder, the hungry look in her eyes as she stroked her fingers down the length of his shaft nearly drove him mad. The heat in her eyes as she looked at his cock beneath the thin material nearly made Julian come where he stood.

He'd been delighted and astonished to watch her walk into the study, still clearly a little weak, her face a little pale, but on her feet and under her own power. Her resilience and strength surprised him, gave him hope that this might indeed work. The look on her face, the light in her eyes as he'd gone to her gave him more than hope. To feel her mouth beneath his, as hot and avid as his own, gave him still more. The feel of her firm body against his was intoxicating. He remembered all too well how tight she had been around his cock, how hot and wet, her pussy clenching around him.

But this...

Her fingers touched the crown of his cock, traced it beneath the silk of his pants, and slipped over the bead of pre-cum. It felt wonderful. She reached for the drawstring. His cock was rigid, throbbing.

"Rafi," he said.

She looked up at him, those intense blue eyes bright. "I don't feel that bad, Julian." Her gaze turned mischievous. "Besides, I want to taste you."

Every muscle in Julian's body seemed to lock at her words, at the image in his mind, at the thought of her lovely mouth around his cock, sucking him.

Abruptly, those stormy eyes closed as she gasped then quivered.

Behind her Nico grinned. "She truly doesn't feel bad, Julian."

The scent of her arousal came to him. Now Julian understood the shudder. He gave Nico a look. They really should wait, give her time to recover.

A tug distracted him, and he looked down to find Rafi pulling the waist of his pants down. Sliding her hand over his shaft, she curled her fingers around his cock. Her gaze rose and fixed on his, her eyelids fluttering a little. As he watched Nico's hand slide beneath the dress, stroking once more, he understood. Just the thought that Nico was finger-fucking her beneath her dress made him harder.

Julian gave up.

His cock swelled in her hand as he reached out to grab a handful of her hair and dragged her mouth to his.

Rafi was in heaven, caught between them as Julian's mouth devoured hers, his long, thick cock throbbing in her hand as she pumped it. Nico's arm spanned her waist, holding her tight against him as he ground his cock on her ass, his free hand beneath her skirt, fingers gliding over her clit, down and into her soaked pussy, then back up again.

Hot sensation poured through her as Nico tormented her.

With Nico holding her still, Julian had a hand free to close over her breast once again, to slide beneath the material and draw it out to squeeze, caress and admire. His long, strong fingers teased her nipple, playing with it, swirling lightly, pinching it to make it harder.

She was intensely aware that there was staff in the house while she was being taken, deliciously tormented by both men, her breast exposed, her cries and gasps of pleasure seeming too loud in the room. Somehow that knowledge made it a little more exciting.

Julian's tongue speared deep into her mouth, while Nico played with her labia and clit. In her hands, Julian's cock throbbed and twitched.

Then Julian's arm slid behind her back so that Rafi was wrapped in both their arms as Julian's hot mouth brushed soft kisses over her face, traced the curve of her ear and down her throat. Each hot kiss, each nibble, left a trail of fire.

His mouth hovered just above her nipple. She could feel his warm breath over her hot skin. Raising her heavy eyelids, she found him watching her. He ran his tongue around her taut, aching nipple as she watched. Her pussy creamed as Nico slowly slid two fingers into it. Just as slowly, Julian sucked on her breast, drawing her nipple into his mouth.

She moaned at the sensation of Nico's fingers sliding deeper and deeper into her pussy.

Then Julian suckled hard and Nico plunged his fingers deep, finger-fucking her once more.

With a cry she came, her knees buckling.

Julian swept her up into his strong arms and carried her to the couch to cradle her in his lap. It was strange to have someone so concerned with her well-being.

His cock though had felt like suede-covered iron in her hand. He hadn't been far from coming, nor had Nico, she knew, yet neither of them mentioned it.

Well, she wasn't some fragile flower.

Every one of her muscles trembled but she was hungry for Julian, for his body, for those rounded pecs, for those ridged abs and for that long, thick cock. She hadn't had the chance to play with Nico yet either. The two of them had only piqued her hunger. She wanted to suck on Julian's cock, suck on Nico's cock, and she wanted one of them to fuck her. Looking up into Julian's brilliant dark eyes, she was grateful to be sitting down, but she wasn't ready to stop yet.

Watching those eyes go hot as she reached out for Nico, she pressed her mouth against Julian's strong, hard chest and tasted his skin with a flick of her tongue. She heard him groan.

Obedient to that reaching hand, Nico followed, his cock throbbing, growing even harder as he watched Rafi's mouth moving on Julian, those pretty lips closing around Julian's nipple as he shuddered with pleasure, his eyes closing.

Stroking the long line of her back, the curve of her tight ass while fisting his cock with his other hand, Nico watched Rafi. He could see Julian fight the urge to force her downward.

Down she went anyway, her mouth avid, trailing kisses before she pressed it against Julian's groin, her mouth sliding over Julian's shaft in what must have been sheer torment as she sucked on him.

Julian groaned, his body going taut.

Sitting back a little on her heels, Rafi lifted her head, drawing her hair back with one hand so they both could see, so they could watch. She waited, her eyes on Julian.

When his eyes flicked open, her tongue slipped out to slowly sweep across the mushroom-shaped head of his cock to gather up the pre-cum pearled there, driving another deep groan from Julian's throat.

Nico saw the muscles in his cousin's body flex, his hand clench even more tightly in Rafi's hair. Nico could imagine that soft tongue sliding across his cock. His balls drew up tight.

Rafi smiled, sliding her tongue around the head of Julian's shaft as she watched him. His body stiffened even more. She sucked his cock head slowly into her mouth.

Nico thought he couldn't get any harder but he did as he watched those pretty lips close around Julian's thick erection. Then Rafi shifted her hips in clear invitation.

To him.

Nico went white hot, his cock nearly exploding with the need to be inside her. He positioned himself behind her as Julian opened his eyes and looked at him, the movement drawing his attention. His dark eyes went hotter.

Slowly, so slowly, because he knew he would explode if he went any faster, Nico sank his throbbing member deep into her sweet pussy. She was tight, so tight around him, her inner muscles flexing. It was beyond pleasure as he sank in her to the hilt, balls-deep.

She moaned softly and Julian quivered.

The wet sound of her mouth on Julian as she sucked him drove Nico wild.

Nico fucked her as her head began to bob, her lips around Julian's cock, Julian's hands deep into her hair.

For Julian, the feel of Rafi's hot, wet mouth on his shaft was intoxicating. It took every ounce of his strength not to demand more, not to grip her head and fuck that pretty mouth hard. Not to plunge his cock deep into her throat.

His control nearly shattered though as she moved, offering her beautiful ass to Nico. And when Nico took her? Julian tried not to come as he watched Nico fuck her, as Nico's cock plunged into that silken sheath. The feel of her mouth around his own erection was delicious. Maddening.

Watching her lips slide over the head of his cock, her lovely eyes closed, one hand curled around his shaft or caressing and cupping his balls, shredded his precarious control.

Then she looked up at him, her gaze sultry as she took a deep breath and swallowed him deep, so deep he could feel her throat muscles working around his cock head as she sucked him.

His control snapped, shattered completely. Julian locked his hands in her hair as he drove his cock deep into her mouth and fucked it.

Rafi knew the moment Julian's control broke and quickly took a deep breath as his hands tightened, his cock plunging deep into her mouth. She heard Nico's swift intake of breath, knew he watched, his hardness spearing her pussy, his hips slamming against her, driving his cock against her g-spot. His hand came around her hips to find her clit. She almost sobbed with the pleasure of it as he pinched and tugged on it as she sucked wildly on Julian's driving cock.

Pleasure poured through her. She moaned. Nico's expert fingers sent her over the edge, making her cry out around Julian's thrusting cock.

Julian's cock swelled in her mouth in response to her moan, pulsed. With a deep groan he erupted, his hot cum gushing down her throat and she swallowed frantically, taking him as Nico hammered into her pussy. With a shout, Nico filled her with his cum as well, spurting into her, his hips jerking against her as his cock emptied.

With an effort even she could see, Julian hauled her up into his arms, his body still shuddering. Nico braced himself before lifting her legs and sliding onto the couch to join them.

For a moment, none of them could speak.

Julian chuckled. "So, I take it you'll be staying?"

Clearing her throat again, she said, reasonably, "I'm willing to give it a try if you are."

"Oh," Julian said, lifting an eyebrow. "I think we're more than satisfied with the arrangement."

He looked at Nico, who grinned.

"Most definitely."

Chapter Seven

"WELL," SASHA SAID, as he settled at his desk to check in before they went out to follow up on a few cases, "you look relaxed."

Thinking about her 'weekend', the two days her schedule left free, to her astonishment Rafi found herself blushing like a teenager as she tried to restrain a grin.

In the end they'd decided she would move in with Julian and Nico.

As usual, Julian had taken care of everything. People were sent to her apartment to pack it up and clean it. Even as someone saddled up the horses Gordon and the staff were rearranging the furniture and unpacking for her.

To celebrate, they'd finally taken that tour of Julian and Nico's property, Julian explaining how to tell the difference between one type of grapevine from another by the leaves and somehow making it interesting. As with everything with Julian, the property was large, large enough for a good-sized lake for irrigation and water. The lake was hidden within woods. For every acre Julian had under vine, he had another he was restoring to original habitat.

They'd taken bottles of champagne with them and a picnic basket. One of the bottles had been allowed to fountain over her naked body, the sparkling golden liquid cold and tingling on her skin. Then Julian and Nico had licked up every drop of it. They'd had fun at the lake. And just about everywhere else. She was insatiable when they were around, which was just as well, as they were the same around her.

Sasha sat back, grinning madly. "I'm guessing it went well."

"Something like that," Rafi said, laughing, lowering her head to her desk to try to hide her flaming face. She was still a little sore, and not just from horseback riding.

Truth was, it was going very well.

"Enjoyed yourself, did you?" Sasha teased, snickering.

"Oh, stop Sash," Rafi said, "I'll tell you all the details later."

The Captain's door opened. "People."

Heads swiveled to look.

"Got a heads up for all of you. We've got word on the street that something's up in respect to the paranormal community," he said, his gaze meeting each of theirs, making sure everyone was paying attention. "Another one of those religious things. It's just a whisper, so check it out with your sources and contacts if you get a chance, see what you hear. We need to confirm this and shut it down before it starts to spread."

Heads nodded with varying degrees of commitment.

Rafi frowned.

Something nagged at her, something Julian had said in passing, not once, but twice, that first night. Something about rumors of vampire hunters. These days there were always paranormal hunters of some kind around. The 'acceptance' of paranormals had brought out the worst among some of the more radical religious groups. There were groups that hated werewolves, but that was nothing compared to the hatred some held for vampires. It was a constant battle to root out the worst of the groups or keep them tamped down.

Still, her cop instincts stirred and Julian wasn't the type to worry over nothing.

Even distracted by the report he was writing, Sasha's head went up and his nostrils flared a little as he scented her concern.

"What's up?" Sasha asked, frowning as he looked at her.

She took a breath, chewing on her lip and shook her head. "I don't know, something Julian said. Something about vampire hunters."

Rafi didn't know where Julian stood in the vampire community, but his wealth was a good indication of where he stood in the world at large. He was intelligent and a predator, like Sasha. Like herself for that matter. Was there a chance his instincts were trying to warn him about something?

And there had been a few cases they'd handled that were odd. The Romany fortuneteller who'd been killed, for example.

She thought about it in light of religious fanatics.

"Thou shalt not suffer a witch to live," she murmured.

Eyebrows lifting, Sasha's eyes turned a little more gold than brown and his gaze intensified. He remembered that case as well.

Like many in the paranormal community, he tended to take it a little more personally when there was a threat to any of them. Almost everyone knew someone, relative, friend, acquaintance, who'd suffered at the hands of bigots. Rafi couldn't blame him given the department's own prohibition against his kind. It was hardly fair since they were as likely to face a werewolf or some other shapeshifter at some time.

"Hold on a sec," he said, his look enigmatic, and picked up the phone. "Hey, Sid, it's Sasha. Could you come up here? My partner and I need some information."

Rafi scrolled through some of the department's files. It was amazing, and saddening, to realize how much hate was out there.

The cop that came through the door was old school, tough, capable, tall, and rangy, his seamed face tanned the color of aged walnut, his close-cut hair silvered. The instant she saw him she thought of a timber wolf, a lobo, and she always had. She knew him by sight but had never met him. Sid Barnes was a legend in the department. Now, for the first time, she wondered if that initial impression had been correct. Suddenly a lot of things made sense.

"Sasha," he said, and then a pair of laser bright blue eyes turned to her, studied her.

With a gesture, Sasha said, "My partner, Rafi, Sid Barnes."

Those ancient eyes regarded her evenly and then Barnes extended a hand to her. "Pleasure."

She took it, shook it, the grasp firm but not too hard, the strength in it hidden.

"Thanks for coming up," she said, and gestured at her computer screen. "What can you tell me about paranormal hunters?'

He leveled a look at her.

"Not all of them are nut-cases, first of all," he said, pulling up a chair and settling into it, stretching his long legs out in front of him. "That's the scary part. Some are, of course. Some are just good ole boys who once upon a time would have done the same to people of color or gays but now claim paranormals are 'animals' not human, just clever imitations, giving them the right to hunt."

His vivid eyes glowed with suppressed anger.

"Most of them aren't really dangerous to a mature paranormal of any kind. Even a normal human can practically smell that kind coming, they reek of excitement, of the adrenaline rush. Only newly made vampires or werewolves, mostly young, mostly young males, are in any kind of danger from that type. They like the rush, too, flirting with danger. With their increased sense of sight and smell, their increased strength, they're only in danger from their own carelessness. Born paranormals grow up with it."

Linking his fingers over his lean abdomen, his gaze darkened, and he shrugged.

"The lifestyles of many paranormals go against what many consider 'family values', despite the fact that once most werewolves mate, they mate for life as other wolves do, not taking another mate unless they lose the one they had. The same is true of many of the weres."

A stillness settled over him, old grief moved in his eyes, but his expression didn't change.

"Still, until they do, young werewolves are as randy as any other creatures, including humans. To those who consider paranormals just larger and smarter animals, that offends all kinds of sensibilities."

He paused.

"Vampires are another matter entirely. Like witches and 'demons', they bring out fanatics of all kinds since some folks consider them the personification of evil. Then there are the others, the smart ones, the 'true believers'. Some of those are quite serious, and very dangerous."

He looked at her. "So, word getting around?"

"Yeah, Captain told us," Sasha said.

"And this one, which do they fall into."

Barnes's jaw tightened, he shrugged. "What I'm hearing, little unsettled whispers, makes me think is one of that last group. When even some hard-core born-agains get nervous about what these folks are saying, I get nervous, too. I'm rattling a few cages."

Looking at Sasha, then at Barnes, she said, "We had a case, a Romany fortuneteller, found dead in an alley. Some thought it was a robbery gone wrong."

Sasha gave her a look back. "Except us, especially Rafi. Something about it just didn't ring true."

Letting out a breath, Barnes nodded. "It fits."

"We've got some witness follow-ups to do," Rafi said. "We'll do them and maybe we'll rattle a few cages of our own."

"Could use the help," Barnes said. "Any help I can get."

"Sasha?" she said.

Her partner nodded. Grabbing his helmet, he followed her out to the parking lot as she pulled on her jacket.

Her own helmet was secured to her motorcycle.

With a smile, she ran her hand over the sleek black machine. The Beamer was no cruising bike but a sport utility that ran on both street and dirt. It was state of the art engineering and could leave most other more popular bikes in the dust. So much so that Sasha had gone out and bought one like it. And it was worlds apart from their department issued sedan.

"We have a stop to make later," Rafi said, as she secured her helmet.

Work first, as much as it tugged at her. Just the thought of Julian sent a rush through her.

They had witnesses to question.

"Julian?" Sasha said, settling onto his bike, then teased. "Can't get enough of him?"

Her grin belied her growing uneasiness as she got on her bike. "Nope. The man has mad talents."

"TMI, partner. Waaaay too much information."

Which was why she hadn't mentioned Nico.

"You asked," she said, grinning.

Side by side, they swung out into traffic, both motorcycles nearly silent in comparison to their noisier cousins, which was another advantage. Especially with paranormals whose expanded senses would hear most other bikes at a pretty good distance.

This wasn't something she wanted to talk about with Julian over the phone, not knowing who might be in his office with him.

As usual, the questioning took longer than usual, but it had to be done. They needed to lock down those cases, make certain they were solid. In at least one case, she wasn't sure.

Julian's office was in one of the big downtown glass, steel, and concrete office towers that took up a whole city block.

Somehow, though, it had never quite registered with her just what the office number meant. Their badges got them past the doorman and the desk.

The man at the desk eyed her in her open motorcycle jacket, biking pants and steel-toed department-issued dress shoes. He clearly didn't approve. She just waved her badge at him as she went past on the way to the elevators. Sasha grinned.

A lot of eyes were on them as they walked across a broad expanse of marble flooring to the elevators.

Rafi looked at the buttons and took a breath as she realized exactly what floor Julian's office was on.

The doors opened on the penthouse suite, to wide glass doors with JL Investments etched into them and thick gray carpet beneath their feet.

Well.

Apparently, the man at the security desk had alerted Julian's executive assistant to their arrival, she was already stalking across the marble to intercept them. The dragon at the gate.

"Can I help you, officers?" she said, seemingly pleasantly. "Mr. Lüceanu is a very busy man. Perhaps I can answer any questions you might have."

Her face was a mask of makeup perfectly applied so that she appeared to be made of porcelain.

"Now she's just being insulting," Sasha said. "The badge clearly says Detective on that gold shield."

The woman's gray eyes flashed to him coldly.

"Would you just ask Julian if he's free to see me?" Rafi said mildly, "Tell him it's Rafi."

"As I said," the secretary responded, emphasizing the next, "Mr. Lüceanu is busy. If you can tell me what this is about, I'll tell him."

Rafi bristled at the tone. She knew that in her working gear she didn't look like one of Julian's normal visitors. She rarely pulled rank, as it were, but the dismissive attitude annoyed her. She looked at the woman, pulled out her badge and laid it on the counter.

"I guess I forgot to mention that it's Detective Rafaela Stratford, and it's police business," Rafi said, "but we'll wait."

Her first impulse was to go to the broad mahogany doors and knock, suspecting that Julian wouldn't mind, but she didn't want to make things more difficult than they already were.

The woman sat down at her desk, made a few minor notations until Rafi leaned an arm on her desk and just stared at her.

Finally, exasperated, the woman stalked to the doors, knocked sharply, and walked in at Julian's call.

Through the half-opened door, Rafi caught a glimpse of Julian pacing across the floor of his office before a bank of windows but his dark eyes were on the display screen and the figures on it.

Like the night they'd met he was dressed immaculately in a business suit and a crisp white shirt, somehow making them look sexy. He was so beautiful.

One look, a mere glance, and her heart pounded.

She sighed softly. Already she had it so bad.

The woman spoke, her expression clearly disapproving.

In the next instant, Julian straightened, turned and his gaze found Rafi's.

"Rafi," he said, clearly delighted, tossing the remote mouse to the secretary as he swept past her.

The look in his eyes was all Rafi needed to see. Her heart lifted.

Julian gave Sasha a quick acknowledging glance and a smile before he gathered Rafi up in his arms for a quick but thorough kiss.

"Apparently," Sasha said to no one in particular, "the feeling is mutual."

Julian chuckled and broke off the kiss.

"It is," he said, turning to offer his hand to shake. "Very."

Still trying to get her breath back from the kiss and what he'd just said, Rafi smiled a little, "Julian, my partner, Sasha."

The two men eyed each other, but there was no sense of animosity, just assessment.

Slowly Julian nodded. "I see why Rafi trusts you."

It had been something that had concerned Sasha. Paranormals, with their heightened senses, knew each other for what they were. So just as he knew that Julian Lüceanu was a vampire, Julian also knew Sasha was a werewolf.

He trusted Rafi too much not to know that she would do everything to protect him, so it was a measure of the trust this man had earned in such a short time that she would bring them together. And a measure of her concern.

"Come in, come in," Julian said, gesturing them into his office.

He glanced at his secretary, he said, his tone sharp. "Unless I'm in a meeting, anytime Rafi comes here, show her right in."

Affronted but trying not to show it, the secretary stiffened, and then walked out.

Rafi resisted the childish need to stick her tongue out at the frosty woman. It was likely she was very efficient, and equally obvious she wanted Julian, so Rafi couldn't entirely blame her.

Seeing the look, Julian grinned. "Behave."

Laughing, Rafi said, "You already know me far too well."

"I do," Julian said, burying his hands in her hair to tilt her face up to his to look into her twinkling eyes. He glanced at Sasha. "I hope you don't mind."

Sasha shook his head, grinned ruefully. "Nothing I don't see in the pack."

In fact, he kept waiting to meet his own mate. He kept looking, but so far, he hadn't found her.

"Good," Julian said, and eyed Rafi's hair, the no-nonsense leather jacket and pants. The spiky hair, the length of it secured, but the ends sprayed out, suited her. As did the dark-rimmed eyes. He'd known from the moment that first night when she'd pulled her badge and gun out to lay them on the table, that she was no one to mess with. And liked it. "I like the look, Raffia. My badass cop."

Secretly, Rafi was pleased by his open admiration.

"So, what brings you here?" Julian asked. "Not that you're not welcome, but this seems to be more like official business."

"It is," Rafi said, looking up into his deep brown eyes. "Julian, when we first met, you said something about vampire hunters. Was there a reason?"

In a moment, she watched as he shifted from lover to predator. His eyes went darker, if that was possible. His body went stiff, muscles tightening, although his hands were still cupped around her head gently. A part of her thrilled to see it, to feel that powerful energy. She was reminded almost instantly of a panther, dark and sleek.

Every sense in Julian's body went alert.

Very carefully, looking from his Rafi to her partner Sasha, he said, "Why do you ask?"

Rafi's deep blue eyes were intent. "We got word from on high that there's talk of a paranormal hunter in town."

Like many police departments after 9/11, they found it was easier to go more pro-active, and so they had an intricate web of informants and snitches. And Sid Barnes.

"Apparently there's reason enough to believe the information is credible," she said, looking up at Julian intently. "They don't do that lightly."

"No," Julian said, "they don't."

"I didn't know who else to talk to who might be able to put a warning out," Rafi said, "to the vampire community."

The popular fiction was that the paranormal community was like everyone else, just common citizens with no power structure. Of course, nothing was further from the truth. She suspected, given Sasha's instinct to call Sid, that Sid was the alpha wolf in the city.

Julian looked at her, and smiled, despite his fears for his people. Her instincts were better than she knew.

"You came to the right place," he said.

That confirmed Rafi's guess. Then the import of his words really hit her. Julian was the de facto leader of the vampire community. For a moment the reality of it just...stunned her.

Seeing it, Julian drew her closer and looked down into her piercing blue eyes. He grinned.

"Nothing's changed, Raffia. I'm still Julian."

Rafi looked up at him, at the dimples that had appeared from nowhere, at the warmth and light in his eyes.

She smiled. "Yes, you are."

"I'll put the word out, warn my people," he said. "Dinner's at six. Catalena will be very disappointed if you miss it. She made Beef Wellington just for you."

Chapter Eight

A HAND APPEARED BEFORE Rafi's eyes, turning a single white rose between strong, agile fingers. Warm buttery yellow seemed to glow in heart of the flower. Julian's aftershave enveloped her. Rafi took a deep breath, drawing in the slightly spicy scent of it as she turned her head to look up at him with a smile. The files had been putting her to sleep, or she'd have heard him coming.

"Julian," she said, delighted, looking up at him, aware of a dozen eyes watching her as she took the offered rose. "What are you doing here?"

It was unusual. Remembering the rumors of the paranormal hunter she looked at him. "Nothing's happened, has it?"

As perfectly dressed as always, he sat on the edge of her desk and shook his head. "Nothing. All our people are being careful, traveling only in groups. Other than that one incident..." an attempted kidnapping that might have been a domestic, "there's been nothing."

Rafi let out a sigh of relief.

With a slight frown at the memory, he said, quietly, "I was called down. A small problem of a newly made vampire. Apparently, he 'persuaded' a girl he was attracted to into allowing him to feed on her. Even though by her own admission the girl was interested, it's little better than rape to use his abilities that way."

Abilities that had once been necessary for survival, the ability to exert one's mind to influence another had enabled more than one vampire to escape certain death. It required will and determination, or, in this case, a victim who'd wanted to be persuaded and a vampire willing to do so.

Over the centuries it had been used and misused but there was little need for such talents in these times. Even so, there were always repercussions.

His mouth tightened.

"Now, knowing what he did and what he's capable of, she's not. The judge will plead it down to a misdemeanor in much the same way as those who use date rape drugs, but even so, we didn't need this now. Not with vampire hunters around. It will just inflame those who were looking for an excuse anyway."

Anger moved in him. "The one who made him should have taught him better. I'll be talking to her as well."

Julian tightened his jaw and shook his head.

He'd needed something to clear away the memory, to calm him down. Since he was downtown and in police headquarters... It had only taken a question or two to determine that Rafi was in the building and then to find a nearby florist. Symbol of pure love, the single white rose was perfect, especially as he watched Rafi breathe in the scent of it, her own stiff shoulders and creased brow relaxing. She faced difficulties every day that he could imagine only too well, remembering centuries when law and order had been nonexistent, but some days were worse than others. This seemed one of them.

"I remembered you said you'd be working on old files unless something came up, so I thought I'd stop by and see if I could persuade you to run away with me. Nico and I have a surprise for you when we get home. Leave your motorcycle here if you'd like, I'll drop you off in the morning."

Rafi grinned. She glanced at the clock automatically but knew she didn't need to – Julian had timed it perfectly.

"Sasha?" she asked.

He looked at the stack of files. "Go. I'm packing it in for the day, too."

She grabbed her jacket with a smile. "I'm ready."

It had been a tough day. Some of those files brought back memories of the cases they covered. It was like walking through a mental sewer in file after file.

Signing out, she waved to all the watching eyes, grinning. Most of them grinned back and one dared to give her a thumbs up. Smiling, she shook her head and nodded to Sasha's knowing grin.

Nico's bike wasn't in the garage when they reached the house.

"He's working late. Get changed, relax. I'll meet you on the terrace," Julian said, giving her a kiss.

The terrace had swiftly become one of their favorite places in the house, for many reasons, not least of which was the view.

Raised high enough to see over the walls that enclosed the estate, a low marble balustrade edged the broad slate floor. It and towering yews to each side framed the scenery and the city beyond and below. At night the city and the stars rivaled one another for brightness. Hidden to one side by the yews was the garage with Julian and Nico's wide selection of cars. On the other and down a level was the enormous in-ground pool with its granite skirt and surrounding marble columns. It was like a temple to Poseidon. The water glittered in the sunlight.

She changed into a bikini, the warm air wonderful on her skin. Basking like a cat in the late afternoon sun, Rafi stretched out on one of the wide thickly-cushioned cedar chaises, letting the warmth bake into her, soothing away the tension.

On the table beside her chaise stood a decanter of fresh lemonade and a dish of fresh fruit that Nelly, one of the maids, had set there before she left for the day. She'd been delighted that Julian had given them the evening off early.

It still amazed her, service like that, even after several weeks. She supposed she might truly get used to it...someday.

Julian came out to join her, brushing a hand over her hair as he came to sit beside her. Gestures of affection like that came naturally to both he and Nico. One or the other of them were always touching her, tugging gently at her hair or kissing her as they passed. When they weren't fucking her, which was often. Once Julian had caught her eyeing him, just admiring the sheer beauty of him and a rush of pure lust had flashed in his eyes. It had set off a matching burst of heat inside her. One moment he'd been across the room, the next stripping her dress off before lifting her up in the air to fuck her against the wall, his cock driving deep inside her.

It was at moments like that, when he revealed his power and speed, that she was reminded he was an ancient and powerful vampire, overwhelmingly fast and strong and she loved every moment of it.

She'd become very attached to them, Julian for his warm strength, Nico for the quiet reserve that hid behind his apparent boldness. She'd been with them for several weeks now and liked the arrangement very much.

Looking at Julian, still in his suit from work, his tie a little loose, she went warm and soft inside. Just looking at either him or Nico did that to her every time and time hadn't seemed to mute her intense attraction to either of them one bit. Familiarity was certainly not breeding contempt. Quite the opposite, it just seemed to intensify.

Briefly, she'd considered quitting the job but knew she'd get bored if she did. Besides, despite days like this one had been, she liked it, she was good at it, and it needed doing. She did wonder what some of the people at the station would make of this arrangement if they knew the truth of it, but she was careful to keep work and play separate. Very separate. Only Sasha knew the reality. He was the only one she trusted that completely. As Julian had noted.

She smiled up at him as he bent down to brush a kiss over her lips.

He settled down on the chaise beside her, visibly relaxing.

With a smile she sat up and undid his tie.

He smiled in return.

"You look comfortable," he said.

Letting the ends of his tie dangle, she unbuttoned his shirt, pushing back the crisp white material to reveal his magnificent chest and, finally, his abs, as she pulled the ends from his slacks.

She said, "I am, the view is incredible."

It wasn't the scenery she was talking about, either.

Rafi was fascinated with his body. He was beautiful to look at, especially this way, with his shirt open and just that little bit of him exposed. It was like looking at a present half opened. She ran her hands over his smooth skin, over the crisp hair of his chest and the strong, firm muscles beneath it. She loved the sense of power that radiated from him in more ways than one, not just the physical but the personal. There was such a sense of strength to him.

His smile broadened as she pushed his jacket off and tossed it over the back of the chaise.

"I'm glad you do, I'm enjoying it as well."

She looked up at him, a quick flick of a glance from beneath her lashes, seeing the pleasure evident in his eyes.

Julian wasn't looking at the scenery any more than she was. His gaze wandered her body, her breasts cradled in the bikini top, the curves of her, the bottom concealing the curls between her thighs.

It was becoming an addiction, he thought, a craving for her touch. One he didn't mind a bit. He loved it, it fired his blood as nothing had in ages, but she also warmed his heart and challenged him in a way no other ever had.

As many women as he'd loved over the centuries, and there had been many, none had ever enraptured him like this one, both tough and tender, strong yet vulnerable.

Looking down at her from the windows of their bedroom, he'd seen her stretch like a contented cat and his heart had moved even as hunger did. This time not merely to feed, but to claim, to own.

He knew Nico felt the same. The knowledge that he shared her with his cousin, his lifelong friend and companion, sent a burst of warmth through him. It was also something of a relief to know Nico would be home soon and Julian wanted desperately for them both to play with her. To delight her.

In the meantime, though, a taste would hold him. He craved that as well.

He lifted her hand to brush his lips over her knuckles, looking at her in question.

Rafi shivered a little in anticipation.

His dark eyes gleamed a little hungrily but not just for her blood. A soft surge of emotion washed through her at what she saw in his eyes. A little thrill went through her as it always did now at the thought of them touching her, but the idea of them feeding from her sent a rush of heat through her. It made her damp just to think about it.

They always asked. They never just took, and they didn't always make love to her just to feed. One or both would just for the pleasure of it. With a steady source of blood from her, they had little need to worry about feeding, sometimes going for days on just these little snacks.

Sex, though, was another thing entirely. Now that they could have as often as they wanted, and did.

Nico had told her it was the first time in centuries they could make love just for pleasure of it, without having to worry about feeding, which was one explanation for why they wanted to do it so often.

Not that she was complaining. She thought she was in heaven, to tell the truth.

Julian turned her wrist to brush his lips over it, inhaling her scent as he would inhale the aroma of a fine wine.

She smiled and shivered a little, goose bumps running over her. He always did that before he fed. Nico liked to taste her skin first, a little flick of his tongue over her wrist or throat. For some reason she found both incredibly erotic.

Julian's fangs extended, touched the delicate skin on the inside of her wrist. His dark eyes watched her. Those sharp white teeth pricked it, drawing the moment out. She now had small whitish scars on her wrists and throat from where they fed.

He bit.

With a brief flash of pain, Julian's teeth sank into her wrist, his warm mouth closed over it and he drew in a mouthful of her. A burst of pleasure coursed through her, raced straight to her pussy. Her vision blurred in a surge of bliss. There were times when she thought she could come just from this, from his or Nico's warm mouths drawing on her, each pull sending a jolt through her.

She loved to watch them feed on her, to watch their faces as they sucked on her, enjoying the pleasure they took in it, in her. It had grown very clear too, that it was her they enjoyed. Neither had gone hunting for other sources since she'd come to live with them.

Another soft pull sent a shot of intense heat to her core.

With a sigh of pleasure, Julian drank her in, the scent and taste of her intoxicating, just a quick snack to satisfy the craving he had for her sometimes. The rich taste of her shifted with her needs, her moods, more intense when they pleasured her, sweet like a dessert wine when she was relaxed as she was now or rich and thick as cognac when she was aroused. He loved the myriad tastes of her, the scent of her, the touch of her.

Watching her eyes, he saw them soften with pleasure as he drew on her and that was the most remarkable part, that she so enjoyed them feeding on her. More than once he'd caught himself watching her as Nico fed. He'd watched her tremble, her eyelids fluttering, the moment so intimate, her pleasure so intense it had him hard in an instant.

"Ah, Raffia my love, sometimes I can't get enough of you. Any part of you."

Especially since she could now feed him and Nico with no difficulty.

Both of them also truly enjoyed her company. Julian was delighted to be able to introduce her to his world, to the pleasures of the opera and the symphony while Nico had found in her a formidable gaming opponent.

She cupped his face in her hand, looked into his eyes and said, "Sometimes I can't get enough of you, either."

The look in her eyes warmed him, as always.

Julian saw Nico's dark head beyond the balustrade, coming toward them from the garage. Nico smiled when he spotted them and turned to come join them on the veranda.

Turning his face, Julian pressed a kiss into her palm. "Nico is having the same problem I am. We don't always want to take turns."

Julian smiled at Nico in return. "Nico, I was just discussing with Rafi about your complaint the other day."

"I'm guessing you have a suggestion?" Rafi asked.

Nico bent to kiss her warmly before he stripped his shirt over his head in relief at being able to take it off after a long day at work.

Her breath caught, just to look at the beauty of him, of Nico's lovely long, strong body. His muscles were firm, his abs rippled.

The idea of finding a way to be shared by both definitely had its merits.

They'd played with toys, the three of them having a grand time in an adult shop, finding dildos and vibrators to play with, including one that provided dual stimulation and another that introduced her to the pleasures of vibrating bullets. Nico loved toys.

They'd trimmed the tight curls between her legs close but not too close. The electric razor had come disturbingly close to parts of her she hadn't wanted nicked and yet the sensation had been strangely exciting. It had taken a level of trust she'd given to very few.

The two of them had played with her for hours, experimenting, driving her insane with pleasure, one or the other of them sliding a dildo inside her or running a vibrator over her while they nibbled on her breasts or fed from her. Julian found a spot at the base of her spine that was exceptionally sensitive. He'd kissed that spot while sliding a vibrating bullet inside her as Nico had nibbled on her breasts and applied another vibrator to her clit.

She had come so fast and hard that neither of them had had time to feed so they'd had to do it again. Not that they'd complained. Or that she had.

As a result her abs and legs were much more toned. She was a lot more limber, too.

It was the sheer variety of anal plugs, though, that had clearly sparked ideas in all three of them. It was amazing. Today, as she did many days, she'd inserted one. Having one or the other of them fuck her while the other teased her with a vibrator in place of the plug was one of many pleasures they'd shared.

Julian looked at Nico and Nico grinned.

"Maybe," Nico said in answer to Rafi's question. He looked at his cousin. "Are any of the staff up at the house?"

Julian shook his head and Nico's eyes lit up as Julian answered, "No, I sent them home for the day. I told Rafi we had a surprise for her."

Nico perked up visibly and grinned. "I'll go get what we need."

Julian turned to her and stood. His hands dropped to his belt. He released it before stripping off his slacks. "I'll get things started out here."

If Nico was beautiful, naked Julian was simply magnificent, powerful, his skin lightly tanned and his muscles sharply defined, tight and taut everywhere. His dark hair gleamed in the sunlight, and his long, thick cock was rampant, hardening even more as she watched. He was simply incredible.

Lust and heat poured through her, her nipples instantly hard. Her pussy creamed at the sight of him. She sighed with pleasure and anticipation.

Julian turned at the sound and smiled. The look in her eyes was all he needed.

He reached out to hook the front of her bathing suit top with the fingers of one hand to pull her toward him, her lovely eyes brilliant as she looked back at him. Kissing her, he reached around behind her and unhooked the bikini top, let it fall away as he filled his hands with the full ripe globes of her breasts.

He liked looking at them in the sun, so lush, so round.

Truthfully, he just liked looking at Rafi naked.

She was beautiful with the sunlight pouring over her, her skin like the finest alabaster, the pale delicate skin of her breasts glowing like pearls in the light, her dark hair tumbled as the sun picked out the bluish highlights in it.

His cock was hard at the thought of what they were going to do to her and he stroked it as she watched, hardening even more as she eyed him and licked her lips hungrily.

Leaning forward, he kissed her, her lips curving in a smile as she kissed him back while his thumbs brushed across her taut nipples. He loved the feel of those little peaks stiffening at his touch almost as much as he liked the feel of them hardening against his tongue.

Julian trailed his mouth down the slender column of her throat, pausing a moment to feel her pulse throb against his lips. She quivered when he continued the journey of his mouth over her smooth skin and leaned back until she was propped on her hands behind her to give him access. Now there was nothing to get in his way.

He traced her collarbone with little flicks of his tongue, then her breastbone, until his lips found the deep valley between her breasts. Sucking, licking. teasing and nibbling, his mouth traveled from one full, lush globe to the other, until her nipples were peaked, rigid and distended. She moaned as he teased her, as he suckled her. He caught the bottom of her swimsuit with his thumbs, drew it down her lovely legs just as Nico returned, revealing all of her to them.

Sunlight sparkled on the now damp curls between her thighs, making them glisten. She was radiant, her skin lightly flushed, her labia blushed to a deep rose.

"You'll have to trust us," Julian said.

She gave him an incredulous look, lifting an eyebrow.

He smiled. "I said we had a surprise, and we do."

He coaxed her to kneel on a towel on the patio and then to lie across the cushioned lounge chair on her belly.

"Now, Nico," Julian said, running his hand over her pale, toned bottom, smiling at the sight of the butt plug, "isn't that a sight to see? Like fine ivory. Beautiful, isn't it?"

Nico grinned as Julian bent to kiss each firm, rounded globe, tugging lightly at the little loop on the plug as he did. Her muscles tightened a little in response.

"Rafi, my love, now you can't say that I've never kissed your ass," Julian said.

Looking over her shoulder at him, she laughed.

"This, though," he said, and pulled a little harder on the loop of the plug, "has to go."

It came out with a little pop.

Not to be outdone Nico kissed her ass, too, but then he nipped one rounded cheek lightly just to hear her yelp.

"Okay, Rafi," Nico said, "this might be a little uncomfortable at first but we have to prepare you to see if this will work. We'll try to make it as easy for you as possible."

"If you don't look it will be easier," Julian said, "so you won't anticipate. Just try to relax. We don't want to hurt you."

Settling beside her on one side with Nico on the other, Julian picked up the dual vibrator, turned it on and slid it inside her - knowing by the way she tightened that he'd found the right spot.

Rafi relaxed as Julian angled the vibrator inside her to touch her g-spot and her clit, moaning as he teased her with it.

She was aware of Nico's fingers by her anus, applying warming lubricant and the sensation added to the thrill of what Julian did with the vibrator. Something slender and rounded probed around that tight little hole, the pressure a little uncomfortable but oddly exciting, the lubricant easing any resistance as the slender probe pushed a little inside. It was a little uncomfortable but it wasn't bad as Nico worked it around and in and out gently.

Heat moved through her, pleasure gathering deep in her belly, pooling, sliding through her limbs, her body adjusting to the odd invasion as the other vibrator brought her to the edge of ecstasy.

Julian bent and lightly tongued that spot at the base of her spine, angling the vibrator against her clit and she came with a cry, shuddering and going limp.

As soon as her muscles went lax, Nico gently slid the thing deep inside her ass.

She groaned as it filled her, stretched her in ways she'd never been stretched.

Julian stroked her back, soothing her as he played the vibrator over her clit, over her plump vaginal lips, probing a little, the vibration easing things, pleasure building again.

With a nod from Julian, Nico squeezed the little hand pump very slowly, so the probe within her would expand, stretching her gently.

There was a sense of swelling within her, a growing fullness, even as the vibe slid over her clit. She tightened around the toys a little more as Nico moved the thing inside her very carefully while Julian continued to tease her. Pleasure built. She moaned a little as it washed through her again. A little more pressure built inside her, Nico sliding the thing in a little, out a little, as it swelled inside her and he slid it deeper. It was like being fucked in the ass, although she'd never done that.

She shivered. It was something she'd vaguely considered once or twice, a little more often since she had met Julian and Nico. Now, suddenly she wanted it.

The idea became even more exciting as the fullness within her grew. What would it be like to be that full of their cocks? Which one would do it first - take her in the ass - Julian or Nico? Her pussy, already drenched, tightened and grew wetter. Usually what one man did, the other would. Nico wasn't as thick as Julian. He would break her in gently.

Just the thought sent a thrill went through her.

His eyes gleaming, Nico looked at Julian, sliding the little probe out and putting it aside.

"Raffia, love," Julian said, "are you ready?"

She bit her lip and nodded.

Nico gently slid a lubricated vibrator up inside her ass as Julian continued to tease her with the other.

At first, she felt too full, then heat filled her, the vibrators making her crazy but not taking her to satisfaction. Pleasure gathered. Nico moved the one inside her ass around a little. Her body was a pool of growing need, aching to be filled, to be used, to come. She couldn't even think as the pleasure gathered deep in her belly, turning her skin hot. Sounds came from her she had never heard before, her core aching and dripping wet.

Julian leaned down to whisper in her ear, "I love to hear your pleasure."

Her whole body shuddered at his words, going hot, her pussy flooding.

When Rafi quivered with need, nearly mewling with desire, her inner thighs glistening with her own juices, Nico looked at Julian, who nodded. Nico withdrew the vibrator from her ass.

That tight little hole wasn't quite so tight now. The plugs and the probe, purchased just for this purpose, had done their job. She was ready for them. This was something he and Julian had only ever dreamed of doing.

Although there was lubricant in her, Nico lubed his cock as well, stroking his shaft, almost ready to come at the thought of taking Rafi this way. He reined himself in with an effort.

Nico and Julian had discussed this, both getting hard just at the thought. Knowing how much Julian wanted to take Rafi's ass first, he knew how hard it had been for him not to, but it would be easier for Rafi this way.

Julian stroked her hair as Nico settled into position with the crown of his cock against her anus.

Nico pushed inside her, the lubricant helping him past the tight sphincter. She was still very tight, beautifully, incredibly tight. The head of his cock was just inside her. For him the sensation was amazing as he continued to press into her delicious, nearly painful tightness.

Shivering in anticipation, Nico's cock sliding into her ass, Rafi forced herself to relax. It was a little uncomfortable at first, forcing a groan from her, but Nico was filling her and somehow it was still exciting. Now she wanted - needed - them to do something, to fill her with more, deeper. She wanted to come with them inside her. Both of them.

Full, so full. It was a little uncomfortable and yet, it was Nico...and it felt good, right.

"Don't stop," she moaned, looking over her shoulder at him.

Nico bit his lip, settled his hands on her shoulders and thrust steadily into her as she shuddered with pleasure. He carefully withdrew a little, slid in a little, to get her used to his cock moving the lubricant around inside her.

It was a pleasure to watch Nico take Rafi's ass. Julian was hard as a rock, his balls tight, his need a deep ache. It was beautiful, intense, as he watched Nico's shaft slide into her.

Forcing himself to concentrate, Julian settled the vibrator against Rafi's clit, teasing and tormenting her, knowing just the way to do it to drive her to distraction.

He could see Nico struggle for control as she started to tremble and quiver again. Nico closed his eyes, mastered himself and pulled out slowly.

"Are you all right, Rafi, love?" Julian asked. He gathered her into his arms, looking into her flushed face. They didn't want to push her too far too fast. This had to be what she wanted as well.

Those blue eyes met his and she smiled a little, looking from him to Nico, who was clearly not finished, his rigid cock twitching with the need to come.

"Both of you, I need both of you," she said, kissing Julian, then Nico.

Just the thought had Julian's balls tightening, his cock aching.

They had gotten so lucky with her.

With a smile and a look of relief, Nico settled back on the padded lounge chair and applied a little more lubricant to his cock in preparation.

The idea of both he and Nico taking her at the same time added to Julian's excitement. There were so many possibilities, if this worked.

Julian drew her into his arms as he slid his hands beneath the firm globes of her ass and lifted her so her legs could wrap around his waist. He let her drop down his body, his cock so hard with anticipation he didn't need to guide the head into her hot, wet pussy, he simply let her impale herself on his throbbing flesh as Nico stepped up behind her. A shuddering breath of pleasure escaped her as Julian filled her. Her channel gloved him, stroked him as he pierced her. It was absolutely glorious and there was more to come. He smiled as her delicious, tight heat surrounded him.

"Oh God, Julian," Rafi whispered as his cock filled her, sliding her arms over his shoulders, clutching at him. "I love to feel you inside me."

Smiling, he pressed a kiss to her throat as he cradled her ass in his hands, parted her cheeks for Nico.

"As I love being inside you."

Nico came to stand behind her and settled the head of his cock against her ass.

"Rafi?" Nico asked.

Another shuddering breath escaped her. "Please."

Pressing steadily, Nico slid the head of his cock inside her as she groaned softly, the pressure of it driving the sound from her. Both of them were inside her. It was incredible. Her mind nearly went blank with the intensity of it, the pleasure of it.

It wasn't enough, there wasn't enough of Nico inside her.

"More, Nico, please," she begged.

"Gladly," Nico said, and settled his hands on her hips.

Slowly, he thrust more deeply into her as she moaned with every inch that filled her. Deeper, deeper, until he was seated all the way inside her. It felt wonderful.

Rafi was so full, both of them stretching her, drawing all her awareness to their cocks buried deep inside her.

As if they had practiced it, they thrust up into her in a rocking motion. Rafi marveled at the sensation of being impaled on both of them. It was incredible, especially as Nico groaned in pleasure, his head falling against her neck to press a kiss there. Julian's eyes glowed and then his mouth was on hers and he groaned as he kissed her.

She was so stretched, so full of them...intoxicated by them.

Then Nico lifted her arm over his head so she was twisted between them, her arms over two muscular shoulders, her back arched, giving them access to her breasts. In an instant her nipples tightened, longing to be sucked.

It was a little awkward until Julian's head lowered and he sucked her nipple into his warm mouth while they thrust up into her. It was electric, her pussy clenching with each draw of his mouth on her tender tip, each thrust of their hips driving their cocks deep. An enormous wave of pleasure built inside her, intensified. A moan escaped her as sheer bliss nearly drowned her. Rafi thought she would lose her mind she was so full of the men she loved. She tightened even more, ecstasy building as they thrust, driving deep.

Julian could feel Nico inside her, their cocks only separated by the thin membrane within her as she tightened around his throbbing member, the shafts rubbing against each other as they fucked her. He watched her eyelids flutter in sheer bliss, her lips part.

Nico thrust in time with him, the two of them pleasuring themselves as deliciously as they pleasured Rafi. Julian, listening to her soft cries, thought it didn't get much better. He had wonderful ideas if they could get her used to this.

Hunger filled him. If they came first...

Nico's eyes shot open, knowing him so well it was like reading his mind.

Attuned to their needs, Rafi's eyes fluttered open.

She shuddered. Julian was astonished to feel her as she closed around them, quivering in the effort to hold back her own pleasure. Quickly Nico guided her arm back over his head once again and pressed his lips against the side of her neck.

Pressing his mouth, his teeth, against her pounding pulse, Julian settled against her. Her pussy clenched and flooded around his throbbing cock, pulsing with need.

Julian could tell she fought for control as they swelled inside her, stretching her even further. She moaned, her head tossing.

At the sound of her moan, her sweet, tight pussy clenched on Julian, pulsing with her need, tightening. Nico erupted with a shout and then Julian, his hands clenching around her ass, came too, his pleasure jetting inside her.

It was incredible, knowing Nico was gushing inside her even as he did, while Rafi moaned deliriously between them. Nico's eyes reflected the same astonishment as Julian's.

Rafi's orgasm exploded through her and she shuddered wildly. Both of them struck, their teeth piercing her as their hot mouths closed over her throat and they suckled hard, their arms tightening around her.

The taste of her was wildly delicious, rich and heady. Julian was drunk on her in an instant. In all his long life he had never tasted another as good.

More. God, more.

Heat raced through him as he drank from her.

It seemed to Rafi as if her orgasm would never end. She shuddered, her hips pumping in time to the draw of their mouths on her throat. They devoured her as her heart raced to send more to them, her body bucking each time their throats worked.

Sweet lassitude filled her as they fed, an astonishingly intense pleasure. She almost moaned with dismay when they stopped, both kissing her neck lightly. They stood for a moment simply holding her between them.

For a moment she just looked at them breathlessly, still wrapped in their arms, still impaled on their softening cocks.

Could she love two men, two such very different men, equally?

She did.

Did they love her?

With a sigh of pleasure, licking his lips to catch the last taste of Rafi on them, Julian realized she watched him and something in her eyes caught at his heart.

She shivered, a smile curving her lips.

"I love that you do that," she said. "Savor the taste of me."

That wasn't it and that wasn't all. Looking into her stormy blue eyes, Julian saw the shadows there, the words she couldn't say. He looked at Nico, who tightened his arms around her even as Julian did, pinning her between them.

Cupping her cheek in his hand, intent, Julian touched his lips to hers.

"I love you," he said softly as Nico whispered the same thing in her other ear.

They weren't talking about her taste.

Chapter Nine

IT WAS LATE, OR RATHER very early. The first light of dawn had yet to touch the sky. At any rate, it was still mostly dark when Rafi returned home. She and Sasha had pulled a four to midnight, but as often happened they'd responded to a drive-by shooting early in the shift. No sooner had they cleaned that up then there'd been another call, a very messy homicide. Blunt force trauma to the chest and it looked like something had been at the poor man's throat. There had been no blood around him, so the body had just been dumped there.

Rafi didn't like it. Something about it rubbed her the wrong way. It was an unusual way to kill a man. They were waiting for the coroner's reports but that would take time. An examination of the wrists and throat had revealed nothing but if the victim were a newly turned vampire there'd be no way to tell.

The moon wasn't full but it had still been a long, rough night. It had left her feeling unsettled.

Both Julian and Nico were sprawled on the bed asleep, naked, legs akimbo, each on their own side of the bed. As close as they were to each other as cousins, it didn't carry over, they only cuddled her. Both lay mostly on their sides facing each other, curled around their pillows, leaving a space between them for her.

Smiling, she decided to give them a little surprise.

Careful not to wake them, she crawled up the bed between them. Both smelled of clean male. They were close enough together that what she planned would be possible.

Lying between them, Rafi found Julian's soft cock and slowly, carefully, drew it into her mouth.

He sighed a little in his sleep.

She sighed, too, as she sucked on him. There was an odd comfort in it.

Releasing Julian's cock she trailed her fingers lightly over his sac and the delicate skin of his shaft as she turned to Nico to draw his cock slowly into her mouth. Julian hardened in her hand. Playing with Nico, she returned her mouth to Julian's cock, her tongue sliding around the glans, then flicking it against the tip lightly, teasingly. He groaned slightly, stretching in his sleep as pleasure moved through him. She turned to Nico, to do the same. His breath hitched as he shifted.

She grinned, turning back to Julian to lick the tiny drop of slightly salty pre-cum from the tip of his nearly rigid cock.

A moan escaped him as she took him into her mouth. He was so large. The musky scent of him filled her. She stroked both of them, filling her mouth with the taste of Julian again as her fingers wrapped around Nico.

Julian came awake slowly, his body tight, to find a hot, wet mouth around the head of his rigid cock. For a moment, his sleeping mind couldn't comprehend it. Pleasure moved through him softly and sweetly as he rose up to awareness. In all his long life he couldn't remember ever having been awakened this way.

He opened his eyes to find Rafi with her spiked dark head bowed over him, her mouth around the swelling head of his cock, taking him into it deeply as she caressed both him and Nico. She'd clearly been fondling Nico as well because his cousin's cock was stiffening in her palm as Julian watched. She was generous that way, never playing favorites.

He loved to watch her hot, wet mouth slide over his cock head, working him deeper until he could feel the back of her throat against the crown of his cock. It was an effort to hold still.

He waited and watched to see what she would do next, saying nothing, biting back a groan as her mouth left him to return to Nico.

Watching her lips close over the crown of Nico's shaft, seeing it disappear into her pretty mouth, her hand still stroking his own cock, tightening around him, hardened Julian further. He ground his teeth to hold back another groan as she caressed him. It was a particular joy to watch as she pleasured Nico. Especially as Nico slowly came awake, too, his head falling back in delight as Rafi's mouth worked him, taking the length of his shaft into her mouth, her head bobbing as she sucked on him.

Julian had initiated Nico into the ways of pleasuring women and being pleasured by them. Watching the two of them now brought all those sweet memories back.

The wet sounds of Rafi's mouth on Nico's cock heightened Julian's own desire. Watching her suck Nico, her eyes closed, humming in contentment, there was no doubt in Julian's mind that she did what she did for sheer enjoyment. As she did for him.

Her attention was on Nico at the moment but her hand was closed tightly around his own rigid member. Watching her pleasure Nico at the same time sent a rush of warmth through him.

With a sigh of pure bliss, Rafi returned to take Julian into her mouth, swirling her tongue over the spurt of salty cum on the broad mushroom-shaped head of his cock, tasting him with a smile. She liked knowing she could give them this.

Sometimes she came home too tired, too wired, to relax easily. Times when, after a long day of dealing with ghosties and ghoulies and things that go bump in the night - and those were the people - she was too restless to sleep. This was one of those nights.

She couldn't think of any better way to relax than this and ran her tongue over the slit of Julian's cock again, stroking it over the indentation in the head, tracing her way around it before sucking it slowly back into her mouth.

She knew Julian was awake when his hands slid into her hair to close gently around her head, guiding her to find his rhythm. He turned slightly so she could take the long, thick length of him more easily. He held her there gently as Nico moved away from her hand, curling instead up against her back to cuddle against her. Nico's long cock slid between her thighs, through the moisture there. She loved the feel of him there, the slip and slide of him comforting and soothing. His head propped on one hand, with the other he stroked her from shoulder to hip, petting her, easing her jangled nerves, before curling his hand around her breast.

This was her refuge, here between these two men. Here she could let go of the alertness, of the watchfulness.

With a sigh of contentment, she drew Julian's long shaft into her mouth, the slightly musky taste of him filling her as his hand alternately stroked and tightened in her hair.

Julian groaned softly as she took him deep, until she could feel the crown of his shaft at the back of her throat. She swallowed deliberately, so her throat would close around him and sucked on him, feeling him swell even larger in her mouth.

At her back, Nico thrust against her bottom, his rigid penis gliding between her thighs to slip through the moisture there, sliding between her labia teasingly. His agile fingers played lightly with her nipple.

Nico pressed a kiss to her shoulder as his hips worked in a steady rhythm to match the rhythm of her mouth on Julian.

A soft hum filled the air. Rafi smiled around Julian's cock at the familiar sound of a vibrator.

Nico thought he'd died and gone to heaven. It was delicious, delirious awaken this way, with Rafi's hands and mouth on him. He'd opened his eyes when she moved away only to find her doing the same to Julian. Sharing them as they shared her.

Watching her go down on Julian, taking Julian's long, thick cock between her lips, sucking him in, sent a shot of pleasure through Nico.

Sometimes he would just sit and stroke his cock while he watched her suck him, her mouth sliding up and down Julian's shaft or as Julian sank his long cock deep into her.

He knew Julian got a similar pleasure from watching Rafi do the same to him, or from watching as Nico worked his long shaft slowly into her so Rafi moaned and squirmed beneath him.

He could feel the tension in her body nevertheless, having become accustomed to her. She was always more tense after she came off the night shift. It was simply more dangerous at night anywhere but particularly in the city.

Knowing that, he curled up against her, stroking her as much for his own enjoyment as to comfort her as he slipped his hard shaft between her smooth white thighs. A shiver of pleasure went through him. He stroked her, soothed her. He loved the feel of her smooth skin beneath his hands, the taut curve of her belly as he drew her carefully closer until her ass was nestled tight against him. The full, sweet weight of her breast filled his palm. He teased her nipple lightly, pressing his mouth against her shoulder as a rush of warmth went through him. He loved the feel of her in their arms.

Nico's shaft was rigid, twitching almost in time to the sound of Rafi's mouth on Julian. His cousin's expression was ecstatic and yet at the same time Nico could see the tension in every line of Julian's body as Rafi's mouth on him drove him slowly mad.

Slowly mad?

A grin spread across Nico's face as he reached for the nightstand drawer, quietly pulled it open and drew out some of the toys, remembering the day they'd bought them. His grin broadened.

Carefully, he coaxed Rafi's hips over a little, urged her thighs apart with gentle yet insistent caresses. He watched as her mouth slid over Julian's shaft in a steady rhythm, heat washing through him at the sight of it on Julian's cock. The wet sounds her mouth made were a delicious torment.

Very gently, at the lowest setting, he laid the tip of the toy against her clit and turned it on.

The vibrator whirred and she trembled.

Nico swirled it around her sensitive vaginal lips, back up to her clit then down to her folds again to slip between them and pierce her just a little. He teased a little at the entrance to her pussy, dampening the vibrator with her own cream. He smiled when her hips pumped and he heard a sound deep in her throat. Slowly, he slid the other vibrator into her ass. She moaned around Julian's thrusting cock. Nico got the rabbit and turned it on, its little ears twitching.

Eyes fluttering, Julian groaned and his hand clenched tightly in Rafi's hair. His body went taut and his hips thrust at the sound of her soft moan.

Nico tightened, knowing just how it felt when Rafi moaned. There were reasons some called 'going down' a hummer.

Deliberately Nico toyed with her, playing the vibrator over her tender, rosy pussy lips, then up to her swollen clit as she softly moaned, driving not just Rafi crazy, but Julian as well.

Nico found a certain satisfaction in this, in seeing his normally strong, controlled cousin being tormented this way, his body tightening as Rafi's mouth drove him sweetly insane.

Nico tortured them both, watching Rafi's body undulate as she whimpered and moaned, her hips seeking the pleasure he wouldn't complete while her mouth was on Julian. The vibration around Julian's cock would be maddening Nico knew, having experienced it himself.

Julian's eyes met Nico's, nearly pleading. He looked as if his control was ready to snap.

With a grin, Nico took mercy on him, nodded and slid the Rabbit up into Rafi to touch her g-spot inside and clit outside as his mouth closed over her nipple to suck hard, knowing now just how to bring her to orgasm.

Rafi shuddered with need, her cries muffled by Julian's thick cock.

As her pleasure grew, Julian became rock hard in her mouth, throbbing, his hands locked in her hair. He knew the moment her pleasure took her. Her body jerked with her orgasm and his own release took him. He thrust his cock deep into her throat while she trembled and shook, his hands buried in her hair as he emptied into her.

Helpless to do anything else, she took him, swallowing as he fucked her sweet mouth, her throat working to take all of his cum as her orgasm shuddered through her.

Julian released her, brushing the hair back from her face as immense satisfaction swept through him.

"Thank you," he said, drawing her up into his arms to kiss her.

Nico hadn't removed the vibrators, instead he dialed them up a little.

What she did for one Rafi always did for the other.

With a smile, Rafi licked her lips, savoring the taste of him before she turned to take Nico's rigid cock into her mouth. He loved that she did that.

Julian turned on the vibrator in her ass once again, stroked it into her, worked it so she groaned and moaned around Nico's erection, returning tit for tat, more or less.

Both of them loved the sounds of her pleasure, the more, the louder, the better, just for itself, but also because it vibrated around their cocks. It was maddening, Julian knew. He watched Nico shiver as Rafi hummed around his shaft, as he himself had experienced only moments before.

Rafi had become used to anal sex quickly and happily, since it allowed them to take her at the same time.

Julian found he loved to take that tight channel, loved listening to her moan as he drove his thick cock into her tight ass.

He applied more cool lubricant to the anal vibrator then found the dual vibrator and turned it on again. He used it to tease her as Rafi's mouth stroked Nico's cock. He looked questioningly at Nico as he used the lubricant to stroke himself hard again. Watching Rafi with Nico, he wanted to take her again.

Julian knew Nico was close to coming. Nico smiled, eyelids fluttering, completely unrepentant.

Julian expected no less.

Sliding the anal vibrator into her again, Julian worked it around to make sure there would be plenty of lubricant inside her.

Rafi moaned, quivered, as he teased her with the vibrators.

Then he removed the anal vibrator and angled the other against her clit. He buried his throbbing shaft fast and deep in her tight ass as she came with a shriek. Nico drove his shaft into her mouth as he came. She shivered and shook between them as Nico pumped his cum down her willing throat.

Pulling her up into his arms, he and Nico cradled her between them and snuggled close to her.

With the taste of both of them in her mouth, Rafi smiled and licked her lips.

Julian smiled at the familiar gesture, one she'd watched them do so often - savor the taste of her in their mouths.

"Good morning," she said, a little hoarsely.

"It definitely is," Julian agreed as he kissed her forehead.

Nico grinned. "Most definitely, Rafi." And kissed her too.

Deliciously spent, neither of them particularly hungry, they curled into her and around her.

"Rough night?" Julian asked.

She burrowed against him and Nico for comfort. "Um-hmmm."

After working so late and then giving them such a treat, Julian knew she would be deeply asleep very quickly. So would he and Nico.

AFTER HAVING GIVEN them such a delightful awakening, it seemed only fair to Nico to return the favor. Rafi lay sprawled between them, their legs tangled together. He looked at Julian, who smiled and nodded.

She would have very sweet dreams.

With a sigh of anticipation, Nico slid down her body, coaxing her legs apart, spreading her thighs and cupping her bottom to raise her to him. He settled his mouth over her, tasting her with his tongue, sliding it up deep inside her.

She moaned softly in her sleep.

Nico watched as Julian lowered his mouth to one of her gorgeous breasts to suck and nibble.

Nico feasted on her pussy, fucked her with his mouth and tongue, licked and savored her.

In sleep, Rafi shivered as Nico's hot tongue invaded her, swept over her clit and then tantalized her with just the tip. Stroking, sliding it down to pierce her, he lapped at her juices.

Julian suckled at her breasts, used his teeth to tug on her nipple, scraped them over it.

Her hips pumped, begged for more, for completion.

Smiling, Nico devoured her, working his tongue inside her to lick her cream.

Her body grew tight and then froze as her orgasm burst through her. He drank her in, her pleasure erupting into his mouth.

Julian's mouth closed over her throat, Nico's over her wrist as they breakfasted. A soft sigh escaped her as their teeth pierced her. They drew on her. She loved it when they fed, it was another layer of joy over all of it.

Her sleepy mind and body were awash with pure bliss, they knew. She'd sleep for hours after working the late shift and so replenish.

She murmured, twitching in ecstasy with each gentle pull on her throat and wrist. Her body grew taut.

Barely awake, Rafi wallowed in pleasure. She loved this. Pleasure washed through her. With a sigh she let the darkness close over her again as they each kissed her lightly and slipped away.

The sun was high in the sky when she awoke. The house was still.

Rafi knew the servants were around but they were quiet. She'd become friendly with all of them. She knew Catalena would be in the kitchen and 'breakfast' would be waiting. The staff knew her schedule. She also knew it would be heavy on lean protein, iron, vitamins, Omega 3 and amino acids to replace what she lost when Julian and Nico fed, although she doubted Catalena knew that was the reason.

An omelet, full of the stuff she liked and a fresh spinach salad topped with feta cheese and walnuts, awaited her in the kitchen

"Catalena," she said to the chubby, bustling, five-star chef Julian employed, "that's perfect."

With a grin, the chef said, in her lilting Spanish accent, "Of course, I know what you like, Raffia, that's all."

Of all the house staff only she had picked up Julian's nickname for her but it sounded lovely with her accent.

Pleased, Rafi settled into her meal, as the muffled sound of the doorbell rang from the front hall.

Gordon, the butler, came into the kitchen shortly thereafter, clearly annoyed.

"Who was that?" Rafi asked.

It wasn't as if the vineyard was anywhere near the beaten track. They had few visitors.

"A gentleman," he said, clearly using the term loosely, "by the name of Bartholomew Holbrooke insisted on speaking to someone in charge rather rudely. I told him neither Mr. Lǔceanu or Mr. Constantine were present, and he left."

Something was ringing alarm bells in the back of Rafi's mind.

She was already moving before Gordon stopped speaking but the car was long gone.

Pulling her cell phone out of her pocket, she speed-dialed. "Sasha? I need to talk to Sid."

Maybe it was nothing. A vacuum cleaner salesmen.

And maybe it wasn't.

"Ask him about a man named Holbrooke. Bartholomew Holbrooke."

Chapter Ten

WALKING INTO HEADQUARTERS to find Sid Barnes talking to Sasha at her desk wasn't a good sign. Rafi's heart sank.

"Talk to me, Sid," Rafi said, draping her jacket over her chair. "Who is he?"

One look at the expression in his eyes and Rafi reached for her cell to speed-dial Julian.

She waved at Sid to keep talking even as she listened to Julian's phone ring and then switch to voicemail.

A part of her already knew, had expected it.

"Holbrooke is bad news, Rafi, a self-proclaimed vampire hunter," Sid said, grimly, keeping his voice low. "He's a 'person of interest' in at least six homicides among the paranormal back east. They couldn't prove anything."

Barnes swiveled the monitor around to show her the man's picture as the printer churned out a copy.

If anything, Holbrooke looked like a well-fed lawyer, gray-haired and tall, with a bit of a paunch, but his eyes were deep-sunk, heavy-lidded and piercing. Those eyes glittered. The eyes of a fanatic.

"He was casing the house."

"At a guess," Sid said, nodding. "It must have been getting too hot for him so he moved west. He preaches for one of those fundamentalist churches, an old style anti-paranormal group. He sees himself as a crusader but he's a religious zealot out to prove our abilities are unnatural, that we aren't creations of God but demons. That our acceptance is a sign of the end times. Not entirely unsuccessfully. Most normals find watching a werewolf change shape disturbing, only slightly less so than watching a vampire feed."

"No one really keeps track of groups like this. Freedom of speech and freedom of religion, you know, especially in today's environment. Despite groups like the ones that protest at soldiers' funerals or the ones who helped hide that bomber years back. At least until someone dies in a way that shocks everyone into sanity again. For a little while."

Rafi couldn't blame him for his cynicism. If you were a cop you saw that sort of insanity every day, and not just from the street people. Sometimes you saw it among your own – the reason both Sasha and Sid kept quiet about what they were. As did Julian and Nico.

A curl of cold fear wound tightly just below her breastbone as she listened to Nico's phone ring as well.

"No one keeps track," Sid said, "except some of us. Paranormals. Pure self-defense. You have to know where to look and where I've looked..."

His expression was eloquent and bleak.

"There's some sick people out there. But we knew that."

Rafi looked at them, her heart heavy. "No answer, not on either phone."

She tried not to worry, to wish that she'd told them to be careful. To put them on alert. There'd been that body. Her inbox was clear, though, none of the tests were back yet.

"Holbrooke believes and preaches that the only way his followers can reach heaven is to kill each and every paranormal," he said, quietly. "Every natural disaster, every act of random violence, is God's way of telling them He's unhappy."

Barnes was quiet, clearly weighing his next words. She could almost feel him trying not to alarm her more than necessary but there was no way around it.

"Rafi, Holbrooke's modus operandi is the traditional stake through the heart and decapitation."

A stake through the heart.

Rafi shuddered, remembering the homicide the day before, the blunt force trauma to the chest.

No.

It was a silent prayer.

Even so, against two powerful vampires, it wouldn't be easy.

No bodies had been found yet and no acts of violence reported – in either case she'd have been notified. Or she and Sasha would have answered that call.

That meant whatever had happened had happened fast or someone would have noticed something, like a pool of blood or a body, and called the police. So they'd been taken somewhere else. All she could hope was that they weren't already dead.

Somehow, she sensed she would know if they were.

Which meant Holbrooke was holding them for some other reason. Her blood chilled at the thought.

His golden eyes darkening, Sasha said, his jaw tight as he glanced around the room at the other detectives there, "And we don't have probable cause for raising the alarm."

"Not yet," Barnes said.

He looked at both of them.

"Let's go find some."

Relief flooded her. She hadn't even had to ask.

Their motorcycles were impractical for what they needed so they took Barnes's department issued vehicle.

Both Julian and Nico were ancient vampires, old and experienced, for all of Nico's apparent youth, she reminded herself. Both were smart and extraordinarily strong.

Something was wrong, though, she could feel it.

Julian's office building was dark, but she had a pass card into the garage.

His Mercedes was still in its usual parking space. Nor was there any sign of disturbance. She was growing colder.

The building where Nico had said he was working that day was also dark.

Barnes's badge got them into the garage of the building since he was driving.

Nico's motorcycle, a twin of hers, was still there. The garage attendant didn't recognize his description as one of those he'd seen leaving.

Both would have thought themselves safe, living in a civilized age where laws protected people against this sort of mayhem. But nothing protected anyone completely. Times had changed.

There was still no proof that anything had happened to either of them. No blood, no signs of violence.

They stopped at a few of Julian and Nico's favorite haunts to see if they were there and had gotten caught up in conversation or something. It had to be done, the possibility eliminated. Sometimes the music was so loud you couldn't hear your cell, as Rafi knew from experience. Usually they called her, though, and invited her to join them.

Even without that, Rafi knew something was wrong.

"It's not enough," she said softly, in frustration.

It wasn't, not by departmental standards.

Both men were adults. They'd have to have been gone for more than a day before an alert would be or could be ordered. That was too much time under the circumstances.

"If Holbrooke has them, where would he take them?" Rafi asked as they drove up the long drive to Julian's house.

Although they were on duty, this wasn't something they could handle from division headquarters. Even so, none of them doubted that a crime was in progress.

Barnes shook his head. "There's too many possibilities."

"A better question might be, where is he staying?" Sasha speculated. "With one of his constituents?"

Barnes shook his head. "No, not for this. He couldn't trust them. It's one thing to ask someone to hide him but it's too great a risk that they might develop a stronger conscience if they discover he's planning outright murder. He'll want privacy, and no witnesses."

"Then he'll need a place to stay," Rafi said, "and not some name-brand hotel but someplace where no one will ask questions. A no-tell motel. Which narrows our search down considerably. All we need is a phone book."

It was low tech but a lot easier to use than the internet, which sorted the way it thought you wanted and by quality. The little listings in the yellow pages were what they needed.

Sasha sat up a little at the thought there was something they could do.

With an effort, Rafi reminded herself again that Julian and Nico were smart. They'd survived for more than a thousand years against people like these.

"Would Holbrooke risk using his own name?" she asked as they walked into the house.

Taking a breath, Barnes considered it. "Possibly. He's known back east but not here. He might feel safer and he wouldn't want it to look as if he were hiding, as if there was something he was ashamed of. Besides, no one here knows his name."

It was a risk calling places like these motels just with a description. The chance existed that if Holbrooke was alerted, he might just kill Julian and Nico outright rather than risk arrest and imprisonment.

They couldn't use their police connections, not without proof the two men had met with foul play but that still left them with good old-fashioned police work. Rafi pulled out the phone book, opened it to hotels and motels and the three of them got to work. They called one by one until they finally hit the jackpot. Barnes asked to be connected to Holbrooke's room but no one answered.

He shook his head. "So, how do you want to handle this?"

"There are other ways," she said, "but most will be even more dangerous for Julian and Nico. We have to get Holbrooke to take us to them. He probably doesn't know I'm a cop."

Both men gave her their full attention. It was clear they had a pretty good idea what she had in mind.

Sasha spoke softly. "Bait."

He didn't like it but he also knew their options were limited. As was their time. If Holbrooke had them, he wouldn't wait very long.

"You can't go in there unarmed," Sasha said, firmly.

Rafi smiled at him crookedly. "I won't, thanks to my time in Vice and Narcotics.

She'd worked her way up through the ranks and divisions, always with her detective's shield in mind. Most of her career had been spent undercover.

In her mind's eye, she could see their faces, Julian, Nico. Her heart wrenched and she fought the pain and fear. Neither would help.

Debating a number of possibilities, Rafi chose Julian's dark green Jag, the least conspicuous of his cars. Barnes's department issued vehicle would be spotted for what it was almost instantly, but the Jag wouldn't be so unexpected. Most of the residents would assume it belonged to a john.

Barnes rode shotgun while Sasha slid into the back. Rafi drove to the High Point Motel.

The place certainly didn't live up to its name being an old, shabby frame building with nicotine-stained curtains covering grimy windows. Bedbugs would be the least of your problems in a place like that.

"A B. Holbrooke matching our Holbrooke's description is registered in room 23."

She found a place in the parking lot to tuck the car away.

Room 23 was dark.

Barnes tapped her shoulder, then he and Sasha slipped quickly out of the doors of the car.

What was happening to Julian and Nico? Terror shot through her. Her breath came in gasps. Ruthlessly, she locked down control. It would do them no good if she lost it. If they were in trouble, they were depending on her.

There was a soft tap at her window.

Sasha.

"The room is empty. We'll have to wait."

DAZED, CONFUSED, HIS sense of smell assaulted by the reek, Julian awakened and looked around in the darkness. The small room he occupied was clearly in a basement or cellar somewhere, there was an industrial feel and smell to it. Oily puddles dotted the floor and he saw movement in the corners of his vision. Rats probably. Over the centuries, he'd fed on them a time or two. It all had an air of familiarity about it.

The walls were made of reinforced cement with iron rings driven securely into them. Shackles bound his wrists. The chains connecting them to the wall were very thick. Clearly someone had been prepared for him.

A thousand old memories tormented him. How many times had he found himself like this over the centuries? He'd thought those days were over.

Fear whispered through him.

And Nico? If they knew about him, did they know about Nico, also? Was he all right? What about Rafi? Would whoever had done this have gone after her as well? It wouldn't have been the first time over the ages that someone dear to him had lost their life because of what he was.

Even with all the discussions about vampire hunters he hadn't expected anything, hadn't seen this or them coming. It had been a long time since someone had the temerity to target him. This was a civilized society, far more than many. Even so, he and Nico kept a low profile.

Mentally, he berated himself. He should have seen it, should have expected it. He'd counted too much on his heightened senses, his greater speed and strength.

What he hadn't counted on was the weapon they used.

Tasers, it appeared, worked just as well on vampires as they did on ordinary men. As did whatever narcotic they'd shot into him while he'd been rendered helpless. It had taken him down into oblivion in moments.

He thought of all those other victims.

This was too coincidental to be mere chance. No, this had been planned.

Fear burned through him.

If they hadn't taken her as well, he knew Rafi would be looking for him, the bond between them alerting her even if she didn't know what it was. With or without it, he knew her well enough to know she would come.

Shaking his head in an effort to clear it, he twisted his wrists in the shackles to test them. It was hardly the first time he'd been imprisoned. However completely they might have prepared, he wouldn't stop fighting until he was dead.

The door, clearly a new installation - iron, thick and designed to hold someone like him - opened and a man stepped inside.

Tall, the man was heavy and well-fed, his belly thick and soft. His shoulders were broad and his chest deep, his hairline receding back from his forehead in deep widow's peaks. Time had engraved grooves around his thin mouth and etched dark circles beneath his glittering eyes. A large cross, carved roughly of wood, dangled from a chain around his neck.

Julian fought the chains in rage and despair. If there was time, he could break them, but would there be time?

To his fury and horror, several armed men entered the room. Two of them dragged a barely conscious Nico between them, his cousin clearly battered and bruised. It was obvious he'd tried to fight them.

They chained him to the wall as well.

Julian's heart burned for him, anger ran like fire through his blood.

"Bastards," he spat. "Nico?"

Raising his head, Nico looked at him and nodded weakly to let him know he was all right. For the moment. It was a small measure of relief.

One that didn't last long.

"Do it," Holbrooke said, with a sharp nod.

They went to Nico first because he was closest and still the most dazed.

Julian fought the chains as they drew their knives and opened the veins in Nico's wrists.

"No," he shouted in helpless fury. "Leave him alone. We've done nothing to you. Nothing."

Despite his bruising, his evident weakness, Nico fought furiously as the blades cut. Blood spilled to the floor, soaked into it, the smell ripe in the confined space.

"Remember," Holbrooke shouted with all the fervor of the Pentecostal preacher he once was, "They are abominations, unnatural. They're demons, they don't deserve to live. The Bible says so. God is on our side. We must destroy them if we are to return to His good graces.

Steel yourselves against their wiles. They're already dead. Remember that."

"No, we're not," Julian shouted. "No, goddamnit, we're as alive as you are. You bastards, leave him alone."

They ignored him.

Then it was his turn.

Julian fought, too, but in the end they opened his veins as well.

As his blood drained so did most of his strength. He cursed slowly and steadily as weakness washed through him while Holbrooke watched.

Julian knew his body would heal but it would take energy. Energy he couldn't replace without blood. Hunger was certain.

A hopeless expression in his eyes, Nico's jaw tightened in determination as he fought the chains weakly. The hunger would already be growing in him. As it would for Julian very soon.

How many times had they faced this, either together or apart?

By morning they would be ravenous. A few hours after that... Despair and fear settled around Julian's heart. It had been a long time since he'd been that hungry. It had been bad enough before Rafi, but now?

Cursing wasn't enough. As the night grew later he grew rapidly weaker...and hungrier. Very hungry.

He wasn't an animal, though, he was a man, a vampire, his hunger did not and would not rule him.

Julian kept reminding himself of that as the night wore on and both hunger and cold seemed to settle into his bones.

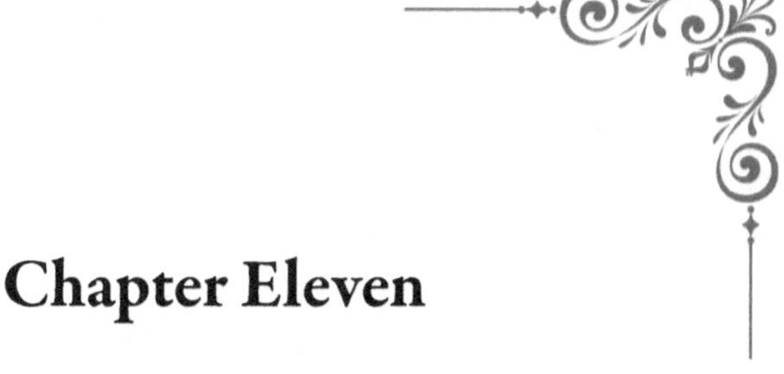

Chapter Eleven

WATCHING FROM THE JAG, Rafi saw a car drive into the motel parking lot. At this late hour there weren't many visitors. She recognized the driver as Holbrooke from Barnes's picture as he got out of the car and the streetlights hit him. He wasn't alone, he'd brought a few bully boys with him. By the plain wooden crosses they wore, they were members of Holbrooke's church. Something about them said ex-military. Facing Julian and Nico, Holbrooke would have needed all the trained help he could get. Her plan was a gamble, but she thought it would work. She hoped and prayed that it would, that she wasn't condemning Julian and Nico to a terrible death.

Though a lot of vampire lore was myth, a stake through the heart would be fatal for anyone, even a normal human. Just the thought of it made her shudder.

Holbrooke and his people went into one of the rooms.

She gave a nod to Sasha and Barnes. Both shifted into wolf form and disappeared into the shadows around the motel. They could stay hidden much better that way, and their sight and hearing would be improved as well.

The sudden mental image of Holbrooke driving a thick wooden stake into Julian and Nico's hearts and then cutting their heads off was maddening, terrifying. Had he already done it? It had been too dark to see if there had been blood on his hands. Was that why he was here?

If they had, they'd regret it. She'd dedicate herself to hunting Holbrooke and his people down like the madmen they were.

She banished the image, scrubbing her face with her hands to clear it.

With an effort, she pulled herself together, got out of the car, leaving the keys behind for Barnes and Sasha as she strode across the parking lot to the hotel desk.

This was the first part of the gamble. She'd spent the previous day in their gated home, so, unlike Julian and Nico, Holbrooke hadn't been able to get to her if he'd wanted her, too. If he didn't the fact that she'd tracked him down to the motel would alarm him. He wouldn't want any attention. With luck, if he didn't kill her outright – which Sasha and Barnes wouldn't allow – he'd take her to where Julian and Nico were, while Sasha and Barnes followed either in wolf form or in the Jag.

Rafi needed Holbrooke to take her to them, but she wanted him to think it was his idea. A direct confrontation would make her seem more of a threat. Then she'd get nowhere. She'd have to be close, but not too close.

The door to the hotel lobby had a bell that hung over it. It jingled as she walked in. The clerk hurried out at the sound, his smile not reaching his eyes. An older man, his hair graying, he was worn down by life, his expression perpetually dissatisfied.

"Can I help you?" he said.

"Yes," she said, "I'd like to talk to Mr. Holbrooke. I heard he's staying here?"

"There's no Holbrooke here," he said. "You've come to the wrong place."

It didn't surprise her. The clerk who spoken to Barnes must have mentioned the call to Holbrooke. She almost hoped he had. She wanted Holbrooke worried but not panicked.

Shrugging a little, she said, "I just want to talk to him."

The man's eyes lit up at the fifty-dollar bill she slid across the desk. "You a cop?"

Gesturing at her clothes – jeans, a heavy hoodie from a local college and running shoes – she looked at him incredulously.

"Do I look like a cop?"

With those clothes and her height, she hardly looked intimidating.

"There might be a Holbrooke staying here," he said, taking the fifty. "Let me go check the book."

With luck, he was actually going to warn Holbrooke.

Her breath came short as a dozen ghastly images raced through her head. Julian or Nico dead, with a stake driven into their chests, blood gushing like a bad B movie. It still horrified her.

The man came back, shaking his head sadly. "Sorry, can't help you."

It was the answer she'd expected. All she could do was hope he'd called Holbrooke.

Sighing dejectedly, she said, "Are you sure?"

Angrily, defensively, he said, "Yeah, I'm sure."

With a shrug, she nodded, turned, and walked out the door toward the Jag.

She never saw it coming, any more than Julian or Nico had, she realized as the pain hit.

The taser was an unpleasant shock, quite literally. She barely registered the sound before the jolt hit her. Every muscle in her body locked up, she couldn't breathe, couldn't move. Tumbling to the pavement, she shuddered helplessly. It wasn't the first time she'd been tased, it had been part of her training. All she was grateful for was that when she fell there was no clatter from the gun and badge taped between her breasts.

Holbrooke appeared in front of her as they tied her hands behind her and snatched a fistful of her hair to force her to look up at him. He wrenched her head to the side as his minions tugged at her wrists.

"Harlot," he spat at her and then slapped her. "Both of them?"

Startled, she stared at him. How did he know?

Then it came to her and she closed her eyes on an intake of breath.

Although most wouldn't know them for what they were, the scars on her wrists and throat were clear evidence of vampiric feeding to those who did.

His eyes narrowed speculatively as he considered her.

Slowly he nodded and smiled.

Rafi went cold at the sight of that thin smile.

"It's a sign, brothers. Clearly, God has delivered us our proof. No innocents need die. If she wants to see her companions so much let us return her to them."

Rafi didn't like the sound of that, or the triumph in his voice. What had he done? What did he have planned?

"I'll only be a moment, brothers," Holbrooke said. "Make sure our guest doesn't make too much noise."

They dumped her into back of the SUV and threw a thin blanket over her to conceal her from view. She thought she caught the faint scent of Nico's cologne in the folds but it might have been her imagination.

As the car bumped and jostled, she hoped and prayed that Sasha and Barnes didn't lose them and her.

They drove to an old deserted industrial side of the city, an area that had fallen on hard times as the economy tanked, as she saw when they hauled her from the trunk.

Abandoned, it was an eyesore, desolate and largely deserted except by the homeless.

Surrounded by rusting chain link fence, the walls of some of the buildings looked less than stable and either vandals or weather had shattered most of the windows.

Rafi knew it well.

Refuse and old bottles littered the corners between the buildings.

A glance at Holbrooke explained the delay. He'd taken the time to shave and change into clothing that appeared more ecclesiastical, including a white collar and cassock.

Holbrooke's men hauled her out of the car, half-dragging, pushing and shoving her toward the entry to one of the buildings. Dozens of cars surrounded it, most American made, many old.

Once the building had been some kind of workspace, a factory or something, but she couldn't imagine what it had housed.

Inside it had the sense and feel of a religious revival meeting. Dozens of people waited. An air of anticipation filled the cavernous space as they dragged her up onto a makeshift stage.

One look at those gathered there and a chill washed through her as eyes turned toward her, the expression on their faces both avid and cold as they noted she was held by their own.

Even worse, in the center of the platform wasn't a dais or pulpit, but something that looked like a large altar, complete with white and purple satin draped over it. Behind it was a table. A large mallet and two stakes waited there, one each for Julian and Nico...and a hacksaw.

Terror shot through her at the sight of them but there was no blood on any of them and none on the floor. A chest wound would have left a lot of blood.

Not yet.

Rafi closed her eyes in relief, trying to block out the horror of that thought.

Hung above the altar was a large screen TV. It flickered to life. On that TV, lit luridly by night vision cameras, were Julian and Nico. Alive. Relief turned her knees weak.

In the light of the cameras their eyes glowed greenish, making them appear inhuman. Both shifted restlessly. They'd been shackled to the walls. As she watched Julian fought the iron shackles while Nico leaned his head back against the wall, his eyes closed, twisting his wrists restively.

But they were alive.

Several of Holbrooke's men disappeared through a doorway at the back of the makeshift stage, beneath where the offices of this building had once been. Some stairs ran up to those offices, but the men went down to the storage cellars below the main floor. She couldn't imagine what it was like down there, except what she could see.

"Gag her," Holbrooke said. "We don't want them to know who it is we give to them."

"No," she shouted at those assembled. "Don't you know what they're going to do? They're going to kill them. How can you allow it? How can you do this?"

Stony faces turned to her as Holbrooke's men thrust a gag into her mouth.

Where were Sasha and Barnes? Had they lost her? Were they even now calling for backup? Otherwise, they'd have a mob on their hands. A mob large enough to be difficult for even a cop, werewolves and vampires to handle.

Holbrooke looked out over the assembled throng as he ranted.

"She knows what they are. Vampires. The undead. She allows them to feed from her, to continue their perversion and to visit it on herself. Unnatural, as the Bible says. Some say they are preternatural, paranormal, a different form of humanity. They lie. The Bible tells us truly. We have the King of the vampires in our hands here. We will humble him. We will show the world what he truly is and then we will do what all righteous men should do in the face of the unnatural. We will kill them. And free our souls."

Rafi looked up at the screen. At Julian. Even shackled and chained he had dignity, that strength. Although his suit was rumpled, he still fought, and he did look every inch a King.

And Nico? Another sacrifice?

The crowd rumbled and the eyes of those nearest her hardened.

Turning, Holbrooke looked at her. "Would you like to see your friends? You know what they are. Vampires. Did you think you knew them? Truly knew them? You're about to find out."

His febrile gaze met hers, eyes glittering in anticipation.

She went cold as fear and horror threaded through her. Something about his words chilled her even more.

"You won't enjoy it. You see, we intend to show the world what they really are. To let the world know what it is to be vampire, to let the world see their true colors and so..." Holbrooke's thin smile broadened, "we drained them. They are very, very hungry now, I'm sure."

Drained?

Did he mean what she thought he meant?

"No," she whispered.

What would that do to them? She'd seen them when they were hungry and called it starved. What would it be like if they truly were? If they'd been driven to complete starvation?

Fear shot through her, for them and for herself. She could only hope Sasha and Barnes hadn't lost her. She hadn't felt the SUV make any evasive maneuvers, but there was still traffic. It happened. Even if they hadn't, against so many and a good number of them armed? What chance did they have?

"You'll see," Holbrooke shouted, and gestured. "Tonight, you'll all see."

His men dragged her through a door that led down into the ancient cellars. Toward another door, this one new and made of iron. They opened it and thrust her inside, slamming the door shut behind her.

Stygian darkness surrounded her.

Rafi tried to clear her hair from her eyes, as if that would help her vision penetrate the darkness.

Only a glimmer of diffused light could be seen, the light for the video camera, but she sensed movement.

HUNGER RAGED. JULIAN fought it. Armed men had come in only moments before. Keeping their weapons trained on Julian and

Nico, even as weakened as they were, they quickly stuck the keys in the locks and left as silently as they came.

Julian's hunger was so great it was an effort not to throw himself at them, however futile the effort.

Every muscle seemed to cramp individually, including his stomach. His mouth tasted like a desert and his fangs scraped his lower lip. He could no longer keep them retracted. Worse, he knew Nico was suffering just as badly.

Whatever the reason for their release, Julian was grateful for it. He hurriedly unlocked the shackles, if only to ease his burning shoulders from their forced position, shaking his hands to clear the numbness from them. Only blood, unfortunately, would erase it completely.

Just at the thought, his vision hazed with need and his stomach constricted into a tight ball. He fought back a groan as he freed Nico from the shackles. His cousin braced himself on the concrete floor with one hand, biting back a moan of pain.

Now in despair he wished for the rats, but they had wisely quit the room.

The door to the cellar opened abruptly and light, shockingly bright to oversensitive vampiric sight, streamed into the cellar.

As weak as he was, fighting the hunger that raged in him, Julian still braced himself to fight as they flung someone into the room.

"Are you hungry yet, vampires?" Holbrooke taunted as the door quickly swung closed. "We brought you dinner. I hope you enjoy it."

Darkness returned but it would have to have been very dark indeed to offset his vampiric sight.

What he saw stunned him.

Rafi, bound and gagged. His heart wrenched even as fury raged.

Both were goads to his esurience. Then he was moving despite his pain and weakness, to gather her up in his arms, stripping the gag away as Nico scrambled to join him.

"Rafi," Julian whispered.

Furious and horrified he held her close to brush his lips across her cheek and so Nico could untie her.

Her scent filled him, as did her presence, their Rafi, his and Nico's true mate. In that moment, tested as he was, he knew it to be true.

The relief Rafi felt to hear Julian's deep voice, to feel his arms around her, was immense. He was sane, reasoning. She hadn't known what to expect when Holbrooke said he'd drained them. Still, Julian's embrace wasn't as strong as she remembered and he was cold, so cold, there was little or no warmth to his body. Nico's fingers around hers were like ice.

"Julian, Nico," she whispered, her heart aching for them and risked reaching up blindly in the dark to touch Julian's face, holding out her hand toward Nico.

A part of her mind registered what it would look like on the screen above, the two vampires rushing toward her, Julian gathering her up in his arms. Those there would interpret his actions as rapacious, her outstretched arm trying to hold Nico off rather than reaching toward him.

Perception.

"Listen," she said softly, speaking quickly. "Holbrooke is videotaping us with night vision cameras. We don't have much time. He told me what he did to you. He's expecting to see a vampiric attack. We need to buy time, so let's give it to him."

"No," Julian said sharply, everything in him recoiling from the idea even as his body cried out with need.

She sensed Nico withdraw in revulsion.

In that moment she couldn't have loved them more, their reaction told her everything she needed to know about how they truly felt about her. If she'd ever doubted the depth of their affection for her, she didn't anymore.

"Julian, love, Nico, my heart," she said gently. "It won't be real. There's a mob out there."

How could she possibly convey how bad it was?

She cupped Julian's cheek and tightened her fingers around Nico's hand, looking blindly into the darkness, somehow knowing where their eyes were.

"There isn't much time. They intend to kill you both. The old-fashioned way with a stake to the heart."

The words were shocking, as she'd intended.

Involuntarily Julian's arms tightened around her, despite his twitching muscles. He looked at his cousin, the image of it horrifying.

Nico was just as appalled.

"I've got help with me but not enough for this. I need you strong, both of you. You are hungry, right?"

Hunger didn't encompass it, he, they were ravenous. Just her words were enough to goad Julian's esurience. If he could have clenched his jaw in impotent rage, he would have, but his fangs would no longer allow it.

Rafi looked from him to Nico even though Julian knew she couldn't see either of them in the stygian dark.

"Feed," she said and then gave them the words that made it all right. "You know I love it."

To her surprise the very thought of it, even observed, sent a rush of anticipation through her.

Let them see, let them watch, she thought defiantly.

Julian felt it, the tiniest quiver of desire and defiance running through her body, the rush of blood that set her pulse pounding. Consent, love, and his own desire overpowered even his strong will. He wanted her, wanted to feed from his true mate. He felt the same craving rush through Nico, his cousin trembled with the effort to hold back.

Almost involuntarily, Julian lowered his mouth to his true mate's throat to breath in the scent of her. He flicked his tongue over her throbbing pulse. She tasted so good and she was theirs.

He needed. She offered. Julian groaned.

Control vanished.

Scenting her need, Julian's head lifted and then he struck, almost in unison with Nico.

Despite the circumstances, despite the noisome basement and the watching eyes, all Rafi could feel in that moment was Julian's arms tightening around her and Nico's lips on her wrist. A burst of heat went through her, shockingly, shooting straight to her core.

Almost involuntarily, her hips lifted.

Their fangs pierced her, and she jolted with both surprise and astonishing pleasure as their mouths closed on her. They sucked. A shot of ecstasy raced through her and her body bucked in response.

To those watching it would look as if she struggled as they drank her life away, she knew, rather than the astonishing pleasure she actually felt.

Her hips thrust in time to each movement of their mouths on her. She drowned in pleasure.

"Dear God," she breathed, "I love this."

Sheer bliss took her. She trembled as that sweet delicious lassitude stole over her and she surrendered to them.

Those words were all Julian needed to hear. They banished the last small thread of guilt that wound through him at using her so. A glance at Nico showed the same relief in his cousin's eyes as the tension in Nico's shoulders relaxed.

Her warm, vibrant life fountained into his mouth. The taste of his beloved Rafi's hot blood was all he needed. He savored her as she trembled in his arms. Her arm tightened around his waist involuntarily as her body arched upward to give them more.

Closing his eyes in gratitude, Julian let his hunger and need for her free. He fed in earnest, drinking his beloved Rafi in.

They couldn't possibly replace everything that had been drained from them in one feeding but that wasn't necessary. Both he and Nico now knew Rafi was their true mate, indisputably, and that made a difference. As Julian lifted his head from her throat to brush a kiss across her lips, he knew it for certain and tightened his arms around her. There remained only one last act to make it truly so, to bind her to them and them to her.

Julian's head had begun to clear, sense and reason returned but it would still be some little time before Rafi's blood did its work on his body, although he could already feel it warming him. His twitching muscles loosened a little.

He looked to Nico, saw his cousin nod.

If Rafi was right there wasn't much time and judging by what he heard – dismissed earlier as random noise in his weakened state – that time was swiftly running out.

They were coming.

"What's the plan?" Julian asked, keeping his voice low.

"Not knowing where you were or what the situation was, there is no real plan. Sasha and another detective named Sid Barnes are nearby somewhere," Rafi said. Or so she hoped. "Holbrooke doesn't know I'm a cop so they didn't search me. I've got my weapon and badge on me."

"We can't make a move here," Nico said looking to Julian. "They have us trapped. The stairs lead up to the main room."

As dazed as he'd been, Nico had been aware enough to look for those details – the kind of information that was the difference between life and death, the kind of attention that had saved them more than once.

"We need more time," Julian added, his jaw tightening. His fangs had retracted at last, now that he'd fed, "for your blood to do its work, Raffia."

Rafi nodded her head, not entirely surprised to find it swimming a little and her hands shaking, considering how deeply they'd fed. It had been a long time since they'd needed to take so much.

"So," she said, softly, "I'll play dead. They'll expect that you drained me dry, believing the myth. With two freshly fed vampires in the room, even though they'll expect you to be weak, they won't want to take the chance one of you might try to make lunch out of them. Hopefully, they won't check too closely."

"There might be more help coming," Julian said. "We just need more time."

While full strength hadn't yet returned, he had enough for that. He sent out a Summons.

Rafi looked at him, puzzled.

He chanced a touch to her cheek. "Trust me. I am a leader here in a way and not for nothing."

Rafi did trust him but thinking of what they had to face, the numbers alone, made her heart stutter. The odds were still strongly against them. The thought of seeing either Julian or Nico with a stake through their hearts, their heads cut off... As many horrific things as Rafi had seen in her years with the department that thought nearly shattered her. She wouldn't allow it to happen.

Footsteps echoed in the hall outside. They were coming.

"Julian, Nico," she breathed. "I'll be right behind you."

Her heart was in her voice, in her eyes, Julian could see it.

So could Nico.

The door crashed open. Light spilled inside, blindingly. Armed men filled the opening. The men trained their weapons on the three of them. Laser sights glimmered in the darkness.

Nico went still with a quick glance to his cousin. A shot to the head or heart would kill a vampire just as surely as a man, as these men clearly knew. Neither he nor Julian were up to full speed yet, despite Rafi's blood in them. It would take time to restore nerve, sinew, and muscle.

Then there was Rafi herself, playing dead now. A stray bullet would make her dead in truth and that thought nearly destroyed him.

Behind the men was Holbrooke.

"Finished? Did you enjoy your last meal?" Holbrooke asked. "Try anything, either of you, and we'll shoot her. If she's still alive."

Last meal? The careless reference to Rafi infuriated Julian. His blood burned hot as his vision turned red with fury.

Pointing his gun at Rafi's now apparently limp body, Holbrooke said, "Drop her and get back against the wall."

Reluctantly, Julian laid Rafi down gently and moved back against the wall, his jaw set in helpless rage. Helpless, but only for the moment.

One of the guards kicked her negligently aside as he went past, shackles rattling dully once more in his hands. Rafi didn't flinch but the blow had to have hurt.

Julian nearly went for the man despite his weakness as Nico snarled in impotent fury. When the time came, he would have his revenge, if only for that.

Looking at Rafi's limp form on the floor, Holbrooke said, "That takes care of one problem."

Just to be sure they didn't look at her too closely, Julian snarled at them, baring his fangs.

Startled, the men fell back, shouldering their weapons warily.

Still weak, Julian and Nico put up a token resistance, saving their strength as the men shackled them again to push and shove them down the hall and up the stairs.

More of Holbrooke's men waited for them there, all armed.

With them, before them, on the plant floor, was a room full of the faithful.

Julian shook his head. He'd done nothing to these people and yet they hated him. Not for who he was but for what he was.

It was daunting.

As many mobs as he'd faced in his life, few carried automatic weapons. His heart sank as he looked at them. There was a very good chance they wouldn't survive this time, the numbers and arms were simply too great.

That was bad enough but he and Nico couldn't help but stare in grim horror at the 'altar' and the tools that lay on the table behind it.

A mallet, large and blunt, the head broad. Thick, sharpened wooden stakes. And a hacksaw.

The thought had been chilling enough, but to see them, to imagine one of those wooden stakes being pounded into his chest to smash through his ribcage, to rupture his heart, to feel the hacksaw chew through skin and bone...

Neither of them were strong enough to fight so many yet.

Holbrooke raved. "You saw them feed, saw them drink her life away. A woman they knew. Someone who trusted them. You know what they are. They're paranormals, vampires, unnatural vermin who feed on the living."

He gestured to his men. They closed on Julian.

"Yet they can be killed," he gestured sharply to his men. "They and their minions."

Julian fought them. Although strength was returning, it still wasn't enough. Even so it still took six of them to wrestle him onto the altar and pin him there, even with his arms shackled behind him.

"See," Holbrooke shouted, "even the King of the vampires is helpless before us. What more proof do you need that we are the righteous? That we are the servants of God?"

Turning, his smile spread, his expression triumphant as he looked into Julian's eyes.

Holbrooke picked up the mallet and a stake slowly, almost reverently, drawing the moment out deliberately. He nodded to one of his men. That one ripped Julian's shirt open.

As hard as Julian fought, Holbrooke centered the stake over his heart.

Julian was all too aware of the dull point of the thing pressed against his chest. The thought of it... of the crushing force required to drive the blunt shaft through his chest, into his heart, and of Nico having to watch, lent him new strength. He nearly threw them off, but more men came to pin him down on the altar.

Rafi.

Holbrooke raised the mallet as Nico struggled against the chains and those that held him, shouting in fury and frustration.

Chapter Twelve

AT NEARLY THE SAME moment three voices spoke almost simultaneously, each with clear and unmistakable authority.

"Metro Police. Put down your weapons or we will shoot."

Startled, Holbrooke's people froze for a fraction of a second at the sight of guns pointed at them.

His voice remarkably steady in the face of nearly overwhelming opposition, one of the speakers said, "Some of you might just be thinking you have numbers on your side. I'll just ask which one of you wants to meet your maker first."

Another voice, far less calm said, "Piss me off and I might shoot you anyway but if you harm one hair on Julian's head, I will fucking kill you."

The first were spoken by a man Julian didn't know.

The last words were snarled.

Rafi.

Everyone's eyes shot to the slender figure braced in the doorway behind the altar. The gun in her hand was pointed directly at Holbrooke even as she flipped her badge open with the other. Her picture on the ID was clear as was the shiny gold detective's shield.

"In case anyone has any doubts."

Rafi's heart had nearly frozen at the sight of Julian on the altar. In another instant, she knew it would have shattered. The sight of him with a stake over his heart was nearly more than she could bear. She tried not to look at him, to let her attention leave Holbrooke, or at the mallet raised over the stake. The despair and fear for Julian on Nico's handsome face was almost as bad. As well as the sure knowledge he would have been next. With Julian gone, they would be free to do as they would with Nico.

Holbrooke's shock at her appearance was obvious.

She grinned coldly. "You should have searched me, you moron."

It had been a rough few moments in that cellar alone. The weakness had been unexpected, she hadn't planned for it and the kick in the ribs hadn't helped. It had knocked all the wind out of her. Only knowing what Julian and Nico faced here, alone, had kept her moving, although her heart had been hammering. She'd forced herself to keep going, keep going, seeing Julian's face, Nico's, in her mind's eye, wanting something more than the memory of them after the events of this day.

She didn't dare look too closely at either of them, not with Holbrooke so close to Julian, that mallet raised, but she knew with every cell in her body where they were. As she did Sasha, making his way cautiously toward her to cover her back.

For only a second, a brief moment, her gaze went to Julian and then Nico.

Even pinned to the altar by the hands of Holbrooke's men, with fear and fury burning through him, his gaze met hers.

Julian looked at their Rafi.

Relief shot through him. There was a chance, a whisper of hope that they might live to see the sun rise again together, that he and Nico would make love to her, their true mate, once more.

Rafi. His heart.

So strong, so resolute.

She was so beautiful.

Her blue eyes blazed furiously, her jaw was tight against the pain and weakness that had to be running through her. That courage...

Julian could see her clearly now in the thin fluorescent lights that Holbrooke's people had rigged in the abandoned factory.

A bruise darkened one side of her face and she hunched a little against pain in her ribs from the kick.

Fury gave him another burst of strength, not enough yet, but more. Once he'd been a warrior and in many ways he still was. All he needed was time to get his full strength back, just a little more time.

It was a precarious moment. He was all too aware of the stake against his chest as he tested the chains that bound him.

Rafi said. "Put the mallet down now, Holbrooke, or I will shoot you."

"They're vampires!" Holbrooke shouted, his fervid gaze going from her to Barnes to Sasha. "Paranormals. Pah! A prettier name than unnatural. Vermin, all of them. Undead. You know that! They deserve to die. You're a cop, it's your job as to protect and serve, to defend the people of this country against such unnatural creatures."

Sid Barnes leaned a shoulder against the wall. The weapon in his hand never wavered as he braced it and looked down the barrel.

"Well, now," he said, laconically. "As it happens, I'm a werewolf." He tipped his head toward Sasha. "So's he. Far as I'm concerned and most like me, we exist, therefore we're natural. By the way, Rafi, I called for backup."

"Good to know," Rafi said. "Mr. Holbrooke, I'll say it again. Put down the mallet. I will remind you that it has never been and never will be against the law to be a vampire. What goes on between two consenting adults is their business. It is, however, against the law to pound a stake through a man's heart. As you clearly intend to do."

Just the thought of it made her heart wrench, grief pouring through her at the very idea.

"If you hurt Julian, though, cop or no cop, I will find you and I will kill you. So I'm telling you right now to back up and drop the weapon."

The sight of Julian with the stake pressed against his firmly muscled chest was sheer torture.

"They fed on you," Holbrooke shouted. "It's unnatural what they do. It's against God."

Her gaze locked on Holbrooke, Rafi was aware of his men separating, spreading out. In her peripheral vision she saw Sasha, slightly behind and to one side of her, tracking them with his weapon.

The crowd grew restless, shifting, moving toward them.

"They did, but it doesn't matter, we were all consenting adults. As it happens, I like it."

Her words clearly shocked the crowd, there was a universal gasp.

"In any case, as far as the law is concerned, they didn't do anything to me, you did. You assaulted them, and you assaulted me, an officer of the law. Even if you did somehow get the case to court on some kind of charge, it was you who attacked and drained them. That's assault. It was you who threw me in with them knowing or thinking that you knew what you'd driven them to. That's attempted homicide at the worst, reckless endangerment at the very least. On you, not them."

"The three of you can't take all of us," one of the men said.

Rafi had been afraid of that. It wouldn't be long before they had an even bigger problem on their hands. The mood in the room was growing ugly. Only their weapons and badges had held the crowd back so far, but it was a fragile hold. They were outnumbered, outgunned, and the crowd was beginning to realize it. They would have a mob on their hands very soon. Despite that knowledge, as much as she wanted to do otherwise, she couldn't just shoot Holbrooke, she had to follow procedure. Or risk him walking away to kill again.

Rafi narrowed her eyes at Holbrooke. "Let him go."

Holbrooke, though, had sensed the same shift in mood. His eyes narrowed and he raised the mallet higher, in preparation to bringing it down.

Once they were accessories to murder, there would be no going back. And the crowd was filled with the blood lust they feared from Julian and Nico.

Fear shot through her and suddenly everything was crystal clear.

Nothing mattered but Julian and Nico. Nothing.

In the small space, the gunshot sounded incredibly loud. The bullet struck the mallet on the downswing, driving it back and Holbrooke off balance. His arms flailed as he staggered backward, and away from Julian.

Shocked, the crowd gasped.

That moment was all Julian needed, a brief distraction as his strength returned.

The chains snapped.

Both he and Nico exploded into motion.

With vampiric strength and speed Julian surged up from the makeshift altar, throwing off the men who restrained him. Sweeping one of them up, grasping throat and a thigh, he tossed the man into the crowd to drive them back. Another he caught by the arm to swing him and send him flying into some of the others.

He reached for Holbrooke's throat as man recovered.

From the corner of his eye, he saw Nico snap his chains as well, his cousin dropping back a little to gather his strength and then drive upward, sending the men holding him staggering backward. An elbow to a guard's gut dropped the man while a swift punch drove another back into some of his fellows.

For Nico it was enough to be free again. Watching these men kick Rafi and then those moments of watching them wrestle Julian onto the altar had been terrible.

Now he was free to unleash his anger and fear on them.

Despite herself, Rafi couldn't help but be both amazed and entranced as she watched Julian and Nico burst into action. Their speed and grace were incredible.

The guards' momentary paralysis, their shock at their quarry turning on them, disappeared.

Gunfire erupted.

Rafi, Sasha and Sid Barnes returned fire, each having picked a target as Rafi and Sasha sought cover.

Bullets wouldn't do permanent harm to either of the werewolves – not unless they were soft-nosed silvertips, which was unlikely – or Julian or Nico, unless they were struck by a lucky head or heart shot. Rafi, though, was more vulnerable. And she hadn't been wearing a vest, as she became suddenly and forcefully aware. She felt the punch, the sudden breathlessness, but there was no time, the situation was deteriorating. Pain followed on its tail, but if any of them were to survive, she had to keep fighting.

With the outbreak of gunfire some of the crowd attacked while others panicked. Several of the guards fled while others fell to the two rampaging vampires.

Just as suddenly, the crowd came to a stunned halt as the massive space suddenly became a blur of dark clad forms, several of whom found armed targets. Said targets were abruptly disarmed and restrained.

Vampires, lots of them.

All motion ceased as the complex was ringed with vampires answering their leader's call.

His dark eyes locked on Holbrooke, Julian said, quietly, "Remember? What was it you called me? King of the Vampires?"

Rage filled him, turned his vision red. His hand tightened.

The man's feet dangled a good foot from the ground and his face had turned an alarming purple.

In the distance Julian could hear the sound of sirens drawing close. He fought instinct, centuries of habit and the fact that this man had threatened his mate.

It was a close struggle, reason against nature.

"Do me a favor, Julian," Rafi said drily, her voice thin, "don't kill him. I'd really hate the paperwork."

It was the tone in his true mate's voice, the faint humor, and a touch of something else, that drained his anger away as if it hadn't been.

Sasha had never seen a vampire in full fury. Then, just as suddenly, it was gone. He holstered his weapon as Julian slowly lowered Holbrooke to the ground, glancing at his partner in surprise when she didn't step forward to help him cuff the man.

His breath caught.

"Oh God...Rafi...?" Sasha whispered.

With a sigh, Rafi looked down at the blood spreading beneath her hand.

The adrenaline was wearing off. More shocking pain followed in its wake.

Almost in surprise, she said, "Oh, hell."

Chapter Thirteen

AT THE SOUND OF THAT soft oath, Julian turned to look at her, cold fear running through him as Sasha caught Rafi and eased her down to the stage. All he could see was the spreading stain below her breastbone. So bright, so red. All he was certain of was that she couldn't survive it. His heart went still.

"I've got him," a grim, laconic voice at Julian's elbow said, not unkindly. "Go take care of her."

Julian looked at the tall, lean werewolf. This must be the Sid Barnes Rafi had spoken of then. Rafi had trusted him with her life and theirs. As would he.

"Let him go, Julian," Barnes repeated, evenly, "I'll take care of him."

It was as if the man whose throat Julian held didn't exist, although Holbrooke gasped and choked, kicked and struggled.

Nodding, Julian released him.

Barnes caught Holbrooke's arm before the man fell.

Looking at his people, Julian said, "Don't harm any of them but get them away from us, I don't want them to see this. The rest, attend me."

The vampires swept their charges away, surrounded them, dark eyes or light fixed upon those they held prisoner.

A look was all it took for Rafi's partner to release her into Julian's arms as he went to a crouch beside them. He knew Sasha understood, it would have been the same if it had been his mate.

Nico pressed his wadded-up shirt against Rafi's wound. His eyes were grief-stricken.

Julian looked up at Sasha. "I know you're her friend but in this you must trust me. We need some privacy and you might not want to watch."

Looking at him, at what was in his eyes, Sasha nodded.

They'd met a few times with Rafi, gone out for drinks together. The ancient vampire had even opened up his land for Sasha to hunt, to let his true nature free, something he couldn't do in the city or, for that matter, in very many places these days. He trusted Julian.

And Rafi loved him.

Sasha dropped a hand on Julian's shoulder in comfort, then went to help Sid handcuff the prisoner, passing through the circle of vampires that now closed around Julian, Rafi and Nico.

Julian cradled Rafi in his arms.

Her eyes were closed, her face as pale as milk. His heart ached. He'd hoped to do this at another time, under better circumstances, but it would be now whether he wanted it or not.

He looked to his cousin. Nico nodded, his fear for Rafi clear in his eyes.

"Rafi," Julian said, softly, commandingly, looking down at her, willing her to open her eyes. He needed her consent.

With a clear effort, Rafi's deep blue eyes opened, brightened as her hand tightened a little on Nico's fingers, her other hand going to Julian's face. Her fingers were cold. Rafi was never cold. That sent a chill through him. She didn't have enough of her own blood running through her to keep her warm.

Rafi smiled a little to see them.

Safe, they were safe. Relief ran through her. They were alive and safe.

She was so weak, though. Her heart thundered in her ears. Pain washed over her in waves, each one stronger than the last. She knew she was dying. Grief tightened her throat at she looked at the two men she loved most.

"Julian," she whispered. "Nico."

"Hush," Julian said, cupping her cheek. "Rafi, love, will you marry us?"

"What?" she answered, frowning, bewildered.

"Raffia, my love," Julian said, "Will you marry us?"

Her mouth twitched a little, her eyes sparkling but regretful. "In a heartbeat. Sorry, bad pun. Can't, though, not legal."

"Whether you know it or not, you are our true mate. It's a thing of our people. Vampire marriage."

Her gaze went to him, frowning at first, and then, eyes widening, she looked at Nico.

"Oh," she breathed.

She looked back at him again, seeing the truth of it in his eyes.

"Yes," she said. "Love you...both of you."

Taking a breath, Julian nodded. "You have to drink from us, Rafi. Both of us."

Just the thought of it sent a rush of pleasure through him. He wished they could've done this properly but there was always later. If this worked. There was a chance it might not.

Knowing what was needed, one of his people handed Nico a pocketknife.

Rafi blinked in confusion, her lovely blue eyes widening, her lips parting on a gasp of surprise.

It was enough.

Quickly, Nico nicked Julian's jugular and Julian raised her to press her mouth against his throat, against the wound there, his hand cradling her head. With her mouth against it, she had no choice except to swallow. Julian felt her lips move on his throat and a shot of heat speared deep into his groin. If this had been done properly, they would have pleasured her for hours and then taken her afterwards. Somehow, oddly, given who she was, this was more appropriate. She was their Rafi, their cop.

Julian's blood gushed into Rafi's mouth, hot and warm, whether she wanted to take it or not.

As the taste of him filled her, she suddenly found she did want it, wanted him, craved the taste of him as it filled her. That first mouthful sent an incredible rush of desire and astonishing pleasure through her, nearly blinding in its intensity. He didn't taste coppery but potent, rich, so strong, like a well-aged scotch. Magnificent. Heady. It was no wonder she loved him so much.

She slid a hand around his neck to savor him, the feel of his powerful body against hers. Beneath her hand, she could feel the strong muscles of his chest, his smooth satiny skin.

Julian. Her strong, proud Julian.

Her mouth closed on him as she fed, sucking weakly at first and then with greater strength.

Julian's mind went blank as astonishing pleasure burst through him. He'd never felt anything like it. He lost himself in it. Delirious, he thought he'd lost his mind, as well. Pleasure washed through him in waves as Rafi's mouth drew on him. It was like a seemingly endless orgasm. His cock went rigid, his body went tight, quivering. Curling his arms around Rafi more tightly, he pressed her mouth against his throat to lose himself more deeply in the feel of it on him. In all his long life he'd never done this with any other. Now he was glad he hadn't.

Nico steadied them, his arms around them. Julian wished it could go on forever but Nico hadn't had enough time to fully recover either and Rafi needed to be joined to Nico as well. She belonged to both of them.

With an effort, Julian fought, strained for control and said, "Enough, Rafi, lick it so it will close, as you've seen us do."

Obediently, she did.

He shivered at the touch of her tongue sliding over his skin.

"Julian," she whispered, licking her lips to taste him on them. "So lovely."

Her words swept through him and his cock stiffened even more. It made him shudder with ecstasy to see her lick the last taste of him from her lips. He wanted to make love to her nearly desperately.

Instead, he passed her to Nico, who curled her into his arms with her mouth close to his throat, smiling in anticipation.

Julian started to say something, to warn him, but there was no way to prepare Nico for what he was about to experience, if it was anything like to what he had.

Cupping Rafi's head in his hand, Nico nodded to Julian and turned his own head to expose his throat.

Julian nicked it and Nico swiftly put Rafi's mouth to the wound.

A moment and then Nico shivered. His cousin's eyes drifted closed and Julian knew Nico understood completely.

No encouragement was necessary. Having learned her lesson from Julian, Rafi's mouth closed on Nico's throat and she drew on him, one long, slow mouthful, her eyes closed in bliss.

The sensation of it took Nico like a brilliant burst of light, like lightning, glorious and vivid, just like his Rafi, their Rafaela. Nothing in his life had ever felt so good. Enraptured, he trembled with pleasure as she suckled at him, pressing her mouth against him so she would take more. A part of him wanted her to drink from him forever, ecstasy quivering in his gut, tugging deep, making his dick as hard as steel. He wanted to take her, to join with Julian to make love to her.

He knew he couldn't. Not this time. Not here. There would be other opportunities now that they were hers.

"Lick it closed, Rafi," Nico said, nearly begging her to do it.

Her lips curved in a smile against his throat and he fell in love with her all over again. Her tongue slipped lightly over his throat and he nearly came from that alone.

Nico shivered at the touch of Rafi's lips, her tongue.

This was Nico, her beloved Nico. Rafi loved him as completely as she did Julian. The hot warm taste of him filled her, slightly sweet, as creamy as an excellent sherry or Irish cream. Warm, wonderful, and delicious. She feasted on the taste of him.

Obediently, she did as she was told.

Carefully, Julian lifted the wadded compress from the wound. All that remained of it was a puckered mark to show where the bullet had struck her. Bending his head, he kissed it, then looked at her.

Cradled now in their arms, Rafi looked up at them. Color bloomed in her cheeks, her eyes looked less hollow, less drawn. Already the change was taking place.

It was good to be King, sometimes.

The sirens closed, came to a stop. Car doors opened and closed. Spotlights lit the building.

Sid Barnes strode to the doorway, holding his badge up so those outside could see it.

"Barnes, Metro PD, coming out," he shouted.

Rafi took a breath, all her nerves alive and sparking it seemed.

Julian and Nico rose to their feet, each offering her a hand to bring her to her feet as well.

Rafi sighed. "My Captain is going to love this."

Chapter Fourteen

THE CAPTAIN HADN'T liked it, in fact he'd been furious. Rafi had gone way off the reservation, taking Sasha and Sid Barnes with her. It had been sheer luck, he'd said, that it had come out the way it had. He had no idea how true that was.

Rafi had faced demotion at best, being removed from the force at worst...until the various law enforcement agencies started to put the pieces together.

With Holbrooke's modus operandi established from his attack on Julian and Nico, they'd been able to tie him to the six known dead and more. From papers in Holbrooke's room, they learned Holbrooke had been working himself and his people up to similar attacks across the country. Given the precarious state of paranormal affairs, with many still uneasy at their presence, it would have been disastrous. It had taken Rafi's involvement with Julian and Nico to catch him. The paranormal community was extremely grateful, especially the various leaders of the vampire community. Including Julian.

Firing her then would have been political suicide.

Instead, they'd give her a medal. And some time off. Which she was now thoroughly enjoying.

Sunlight bathed her skin in warmth as Julian's lips touched the small puckered scar below and just beneath her breasts. It was a weekend so the servants had the time off. She, Julian, and Nico had the entire house to themselves.

Nico was living out his fantasy and Rafi was happy to oblige.

She was awash in sensation, bound with silk scarves by her wrists and ankles to one of the large cedar chaises on the terrace. The sweet scent of summer was all around her while Julian and Nico played with her. The scarves were all she wore, they were all any of them wore. Warm sun drenched them as well, Julian magnificent in his nakedness, Nico beautiful.

Rafi had never dared to dream of anything like this.

Slowly Nico slid a slender well-lubricated bullet up her ass where it hummed inside her maddeningly. Her pussy flexed around another. Nico did like his toys. She whimpered as he teased her clit with a vibrator until she trembled. Warming lubricant only made the sensations more intense.

Julian licked and sucked at her nipple, slid his tongue around her aureole, nibbled at the taut tip while he plumped and caressed her other breast with his free hand. He pinched that tender nub, tugged at it.

He loved this. Nothing else mattered but Rafi and Nico. They loved toying with her, finding new ways of pleasuring her. Each time made the next that much better.

The remote-controlled bullets slowly increased the speed of their vibrations as Nico dialed them up. Rafi went beyond thought. There was only the pleasure that built inside her until her body was wound tight with need. A soft mouth replaced the vibrator at her clit. Nico, she knew that touch. His tongue slipped and slid over her or sucked lightly at that sensitized bud until her thighs and belly twitched to each delicate touch to her heated flesh.

Fangs scraped over the delicate skin of her wrist, a warm mouth closed. She felt the sharp prick just before those teeth pierced. She jolted with pleasure as Julian suckled lightly, tasting her.

"Not yet," he pronounced, licking her wrist to close the small wounds. The soft brush of his tongue was as arousing as the rest.

"Julian," she whispered, almost in a wail.

The bullet in her ass slid out, to be replaced by a thick, freshly lubed vibrator. Nico slid the device in slowly as his tongue toyed with her clit. She groaned as the wand filled her ever more deeply and the speed of its motion increased. He stroked his fingers up her thigh, the touch ephemeral, tantalizing as he toyed with the delicate tissues of her lower lips. Then two fingers slid inside her, to play with the bullet as his mouth returned to tormenting her clit.

Despite all her efforts not to, Rafi cried out, her body straining against her bonds.

"Getting there, though," Julian said, approvingly, considering it.

Nico's fingers slipped out of her. She whimpered in protest but larger fingers replaced them as Nico moved away, licking his lips in anticipation as he brushed his lips over her other wrist.

As Julian's head lowered between her thighs to suckle at the tender bud between them, he toyed with the bullet vibrating inside her.

Rafi thought she'd go blind with pleasure and then she felt Nico's lips brush over her wrist. His tongue flicked, tasting her. Teasing her.

She looked at him. As their eyes met she knew he'd been waiting just for just that. Slowly, deliberately, he bit down and sucked deeply. Something about watching that, watching his brown eyes looking into hers as he did it sent another jolt through her.

Pleasure shot through her along with the pain and she arched.

Her gaze was locked on his she watched him lift his head and savor the taste of her, his eyes closing as he moaned with the pleasure of it. She almost came just at that.

It might have been a signal.

She felt the butterfly stimulator close on her clit and the vibrators switch to full power as both Julian and Nico battened on her wrists almost as one. Brief pain and then intense pleasure shot through her. Ecstasy blinded her as her orgasm exploded through her from the butterfly stimulating her clit as Julian and Nico feasted. Her body bowed and went rigid, trembling. She cried out in bliss as they drank, slowly, savoring her, drawing out her pleasure until she thought she'd lose her mind. It seemed to go on forever, that orgasm, her heart pounding wildly as it washed through her in waves.

The taste of Rafi's pleasure in Julian's mouth was better than the finest wine, almost effervescent and Julian reveled in the rich heady taste of her. He let her fill him, heart and soul, he breathed the scent of it and her in, filled himself with her.

All the rough edges, the fears and fury of the last few days washed away.

He let out a sigh, as he lifted his mouth from her, still savoring the taste of her in his mouth, and looked at the color of her pleasure, the soft blush of ecstasy wash through her skin. Her lovely eyes were closed, her body taut as Nico fed.

Rapt in the taste of her, of their beloved Rafi, Nico just drew her in, a mouthful at a time as he increased the speed on the butterfly until she whimpered, her body shuddering helplessly. Her pleasure was glorious to feel...and taste. He rolled that taste on his tongue, his cock hot and hard. It would grow harder. He couldn't wait to fill her, to fuck her. They'd come far too close to losing her, now he couldn't get enough of her. She went limp, eyelids fluttering as her orgasm slowly let her go.

Delighted, Nico lifted his head.

With the toys still inside her, he and Julian released her from her silken bonds while she trembled and quivered.

Julian stroked a hand over her heated skin, tweaked her taut nipples. She murmured, opening her eyes a little and he smiled to see them hazed with pleasure, her lids fluttering.

He looked to Nico, who smiled as Julian flicked the butterfly gently. Nico worked the vibrator in her ass around a little. Rafi cried out softly, her body tightening again, trembling. She looked up at them past heavy lids.

Julian could feel her blood rush through him, filling him, thickening his cock even further.

With a smile, he gathered her up.

"I love you," he said, as he cradled her close. "This time we'll do it right."

Nico nicked the vein in Julian's throat with a little silver blade.

This time there was no need to coax her. Her lips moved and she sucked, drew on him with a moan.

Dazed as she was with pleasure, Rafi remembered. The taste of Julian seemed to explode through her, strong and rich, as potent as the finest whiskey. In an instant, it was as if she were drunk on him. Heat raced through her veins, to every inch of her body, and with it, intense desire.

She loved Julian, loved Nico, with a force that made her heart pound. She wanted him, she wanted them with an intensity that belied the fact they'd just rendered her limp and trembling. Sliding her hands up into Julian's thick hair, she drew him closer, stroked the silken strands.

If Julian had thought the sensation of Rafi drinking from him had been intense before, it was nothing to this. He jolted as a burst of pure ecstasy shot through him, his cock turning as hard as iron it seemed. Her caress nearly broke his heart, her hands gentle as she held him.

With an effort, his body yearning for release, he drew her mouth away. It had to be both of them, all of them.

Even so, it took all his control to keep from taking her then and there.

Instead, he kissed her, softly, then turned her toward Nico.

Their eyes met, his, hers and his cousin's, and Nico nodded with a smile.

Nico placed the blade in Julian's hand as Rafi reached up to cup his cheek. The tenderness of that gesture as Julian nicked his throat was no comparison to the incredible sensation of her mouth closing on it. Nico shuddered his pleasure, more so as she moaned, and not just at his taste.

Julian was slowly removing the bullet and vibrator. Her mouth locked on his throat as she clung to him, trembling.

He tightened his arms around her as he lowered her to the chaise, his own need making his rigid cock throb. In all his life he'd never wanted a woman like this, but then, Rafi was their true mate, something they'd never hoped to find.

Rafi's head spun as the taste of him filled her, as his sweet taste, his more subtle warmth spread within her. Delicious pleasure washed through her, each wave more intense.

Her pussy ached with need, she wanted desperately to be filled, to be fucked.

Watching as Rafi drank Nico was incredibly erotic, it took everything Julian had to keep himself in check, to do this right.

Nico cradled her with one arm, caressed her breasts with his free hand, then looked up at Julian.

It was an incredible view, Rafi's hips at the end of the chaise, her legs spread. Julian thought he'd never seen her so beautiful. His cock throbbed at the sight of her, of her desire glistening on the curls between her thighs.

Transfixed, Rafi could only stare up at Julian. He was incredible, every muscle seemed taut with iron control. His cock seemed huge, erect and twitching.

His dark eyes were intent on her.

In one motion, he slid his hands beneath her hips so her legs were draped over his arms and drove his long thick cock deep inside her.

She cried out as he thrust inside her, as he filled her.

Nico's hand closed on her breast, squeezing it, toying and tugging on her nipple.

It was incredible to feel every inch of Julian drive so deep and hard inside her. Without Nico holding her in place, she didn't know that she could have held herself on the chaise. The sweet friction of his cock as it battered inside her drove her crazy. She quivered, so close, so close to coming.

For a moment Julian held, buried inside her, and shifted his hips to better feel her.

"I love to feel you tighten around me like that," he groaned, his eyes closing, but he wanted to share the incredible sensation of her. "Nico, feel this."

A rush of heat went through her, even as she gasped to find herself empty suddenly, and then Nico's cock drove into her and she quivered. Her hips pumped against him.

Nico's eyes went closed as he worked himself inside her.

The pleasure of it made Rafi moan, the muscles inside her clenching and flexing around him.

Fingers toyed with her clit, Julian's, and a rush of ecstasy made the muscles inside her tighten around Nico's cock. Nico shuddered as he lifted her hips higher to grind himself inside her.

A mouth closed over her nipple, sucked. She wailed softly, needing desperately to come.

Then Nico was gone but she was only empty for a minute. A thicker, fuller shaft drove deep inside her. Julian, his cock pulsing as he pounded into her. Her hips thrust, pumped as Nico braced her to take him, his mouth closing on her breast while his fingers found her clit.

She'd thought Julian big before, but it was nothing like this, his cock stretched every inch of her.

Looking down, watching his shaft push inside Rafi while Nico sucked hard on her nipple as she tightened around him, was more that Julian could take.

With a shout he came, filling her with his seed, his body locked as he emptied inside her. Her internal muscles closed tightly around him. She came on a soft cry but he pulled out swiftly to make room for Nico. Julian's cock filled her mouth so she could take the last of his cum from him.

Feeling Nico inside her was the last straw.

Rafi sucked nearly frantically, her hips pumped wildly as her interrupted orgasm was completed.

Julian moaned gratefully in relief and release while Nico groaned as he came.

They collapsed in a limp tangle of limbs and bodies on the chaise, both Julian and Nico with their arms and legs wrapped tightly around Rafi in order to fit. It was still surprisingly comfortable.

Julian kissed Rafi gently, followed by Nico.

For the first time in his long life, Julian found he could consider something close to what most considered normal. A home, family. That was something no vampire had ever dared dream about, hunted as they'd been through time.

He looked over at Nico and saw the same contentment and the same hope mirrored in his cousin's eyes.

Until they heard the sound of car tires on the drive.

A little distracted, still in a sensual haze, Julian said, "Are we expecting visitors?"

"You did invite Sasha and Sid up for drinks, a swim and a hunt," Rafi said, grinning. "Something about a problem with deer eating the grapes?"

"And Holbrooke said *we* were vermin," Julian complained. "Bloody deer, they're eating my best vines."

Then the reality of the situation hit him. He opened his eyes and looked at Rafi, sandwiched between him and Nico.

Both she and Nico were grinning. And naked.

"Bloody hell," he exploded, and then added, wryly. "Clothes."

"Good idea," Rafi said.

"Just for that," he said...and tossed her over his shoulder.

"Julian, put me down."

"No," Julian said, with a glance at his cousin, who just smacked her on her pretty ass.

Laughing, they raced inside like guilty children.

Moments later Julian greeted Sasha and Sid at the door dressed in a polo shirt and jeans as Rafi came to join them wearing a gauzy dress sans underwear.

Neither Sasha nor Sid was fooled, especially since Nico followed, grinning like a loon, but it didn't matter.

All of them settled around the table on the patio, looking out over the vineyard.

Rafi took a deep breath and smiled contentedly as Julian and Sid talked politics while Nico and Sasha talked games and sports.

She wasn't a vampire. From what Julian and Nico told her she wouldn't be one for a very long time. Not until she actually died the true death, neither of them being able to reach her in time. If she were, they couldn't feed from her or her from them and none of them wanted that.

The risk of death wasn't entirely unlikely in her line of work, as they'd already experienced, but it much harder now. Unless a bullet hit her head or heart, she was nearly invulnerable. Drinking from them had unexpected side benefits, it had turned her into something of a bionic cop, giving her increased strength and speed, and a much longer life span. It seemed she'd joined the ranks of the paranormal. As long as she drank from them now and then, she'd stay the age she was virtually forever.

With them.

About the author

AWARD-WINNING AUTHOR Valerie Douglas is a prolific writer and genre-crosser, much to the delight of her fans. She reads and writes classic fantasy, romance, suspense, and as V.J. Devereaux, erotic romance. Who knows what will pop up down the road!

And she's on the road - a Nomadic Writer who faced challenging times with grace and optimism, until she finally found a home in Italy.

She's written 29 novels that reflect her eclectic tastes - high fantasy (the Author Shout Recommended Read) Coming Storm series, as well as Song of the Fairy Queen, historical fantasy - the Servant of the Gods series - mysteries, thrillers, westerns, and romantic suspense. She writes books for adults with rich character and plot-driven stories.

To get to know the author better, visit her Facebook page: https://www.facebook.com/Valerie.Douglas.Books

her web/blog page https://valeriedouglasauthor.com/

or follow her on Twitter https://twitter.com/ValerieDouglasA

If you like this book, please leave a review.

Other Novels by Valerie Douglas

THE COMING STORM SERIES:

The Coming Storm Elon of Aerilann, Elven advisor to the High King of Men, helped negotiate the treaty between his people, Dwarves and men. He suddenly finds that fragile truce threatened from without by an unknown enemy and from within by old hatreds and prejudice. With the aid of his true-friend Colath, the wizard Jareth, and the Elven archer Jalila, he searches for the source of the threat.

Ailith, Heir to the Kingdom of Riverford, fights her own silent battle. Her father has changed, but her quest to discover what changed him puts her life and very soul in danger, leaving her only one direction in which to turn. Elon.

To preserve the alliance, though, Elon will have to choose between duty and his Elven honor...

A Convocation of Kings – sequel to The Coming Storm. A shadow has fallen over the Kingdoms and once again Elon, Colath, Jareth and Jalila are called to answer it. One ally is lost, but another returns while a terrible tragedy nearly costs them a third. Now a member of the ruling Council, Elon of Aerilann and his companions, Colath, Jareth and Jalila are forced to fight for the Alliance they've given everything to preserve, even as a breath of hope is offered...

Not Magic Enough - For Delae, a lonely landholder on the edge of the Kingdoms, a frantic knock at the door on a stormy winter's night brings more than a cry for help. After centuries of war Elves have little contact with the race of men, but Dorovan can't bring himself to ride past those so obviously in need. One small act, with enormous consequences. Not Magic Enough is a tale of love and honor, duty and determination.

Setting Boundaries - After centuries of war an uneasy peace has finally been negotiated between Elves, Dwarves and Men, thanks to Elon of Aerilann, Elven councilor to the High King of Men. One final task yet remains, one final bone of contention - to set the boundaries between their lands. For journeyman wizard Jareth it's the opportunity of a lifetime. What he doesn't know is that the journey will test him to his limits and forge a friendship that will last for centuries.

Song of the Fairy Queen - It's said of Fairy that if you're in dire need and you call their name they'll come. With his castle under siege and young son in his arms, High King Oryan couldn't be in more dire need. With only his High Marshal, Morgan, and a handful of Morgan's men at his back, he has only one direction left to run...up. And only one ally to whom he can turn.

Kyriay, the Queen of the Fairy.

The Servant of the Gods series

Servant of the Gods – A child of prophecy, she would bear many names. Born a peasant, she became a mercenary, was captured and enslaved, but rose to become a Priestess of Isis. As High Priestess she would face her greatest challenge yet and find a love that would last beyond time.

Heart of the Gods – When archaeologist Ky Farrar starts in search of the ancient Tomb, he awakens its lethal, and lovely, guardian. Both quickly discover Ky isn't the only one in search of the tomb and the danger to the world that lies within it. The key to which is the Heart of the Gods.

Romance:
The Millersburg Quartet

Irish Fling – Ali was the smart one, but brains didn't stop her from crashing and burning. A desire to connect with her roots takes her to Ireland and a chance meeting with internet mogul Aidan O'Connell. Even brilliant Ali with her nearly photographic memory doesn't realize the danger lurking when she sees the wrong thing.

Dirty Politics – Returning to her hometown, practical Cam Kenyon discovers that teenage crush Noah Denton is running for D.A. When she discovers that his opponent is going to indulge in dirty politics, she throws her support to him, accidentally resurrecting an old enemy.

Director's Cut – When bad-boy director Jack Tyler comes to town to rediscover his passion with the local community theater group, teacher and theater geek Molly has to decide whether to take a chance on him. When his past catches up with him and he seems to be returning to his old bad habits, she has to decide whether to fight his demons alongside him.

Two Up – Sculptor and welder Jesse was always the wild child, her only real family her three friends. A chance meeting with novelist Mitch Donovan gives her a chance to make a new life. For Mitch meeting Jesse gives him new inspiration, but that inspiration comes at a terrifying price.

Lucky Charm – When private investigator Matt Morrison's best friend Bill is murdered, all evidence seems to point at his company, but Matt's every attempt at entry is thwarted. Violently. When pretty Ariel O'Donnell comes unexpectedly to his rescue, he resolves to keep her out of what is clearly a dangerous situation. Unfortunately, it seems Ariel is already involved and the forces set in motion by Bill's death are closing around her.

Picture Perfect - Anne Sheridan, aka reclusive artist C. A. Calloway, finds herself in the middle of a high-stakes game of Monopoly, with dangerous consequences.

Michael Kelley, CEO of Kelley Hotels and Resorts, hadn't intended that when he'd offered to buy her property to build a new resort. That property was ideal for what he had in mind for a new resort. With so much money on the line, now he has to find a way to keep her safe...

A steamy, sultry thriller, Picture Perfect will set your pulse racing...

As V. J. Devereaux

The Book of Demons series

Demon's Kiss

Demon's Embrace

Cherry's Jubilee

Special Delivery

The Bound Series

Blood Bound

Magic Bound

***The Brothers in Blue and Red** series*

The Brothers in Blue and Red: Saving Maya

The Brothers in Blue and Red: Rescuing Ceili

Fire Season